"You sure you want me to attack you with this?" June asked. She held a sharp bowie knife in her right hand.

Levi stood opposite her with both hands on his hips. "Yeah." he crouched into position. "Now come on; go for me!"

The two circled each other warily. June slashed the knife about as expertly as she could. Just as she was ready to set upon him, Mrs. Lynch's voice rang out, "Stage coming!"

June glanced up and, before she knew it, Levi had gripped her wrist, forced the knife out of her hand, and kicked her legs out from under her. She fell flat onto the ground.

"Never," he said, looking down at her, "let yourself get taken off guard like that again. Especially when you're in danger. If I had been someon̲e̲ ̲ you would have been dead."

Also by Rina Keaton:

Freedom Run

The Revenge of June Daley

RINA KEATON

An Original Holloway House Edition
HOLLOWAY HOUSE PUBLISHING COMPANY
LOS ANGELES, CALIFORNIA

Published by
HOLLOWAY HOUSE PUBLISHING COMPANY
8060 Melrose Avenue, Los Angeles, California 90046

This is a work of fiction. Names, characters, places, and incidents
are either the product of the author's imagination or are used fic-
titiously. Any resemblance to actual events or locales or persons,
living or dead, is entirely coincidental.

International Standard Book Number 0-87067-970-8
Printed in the United States of America

Cover photograph by Jeffrey. Posed by professional models.
Cover design by Greg Salman.

The Revenge of June Daley

Chapter 1

Devonfield Plantation, Tennessee, December 1862.

"Merry Christmas, Massa George," June said as she placed a plate of steaming grits and eggs on the breakfast table before him.

June's master, a broad-shouldered man in his late forties with a shock of gray-black hair, peered at her with bleary eyes. "What's so goddamn merry about this morning?"

Fear seared June as the man gripped her forearm in a swift motion. God! How she hated that feeling! The helplessness that marked her life as a slave.

"Nothing, sir. I was just trying to be cheerful." June attempted a smile. It didn't work. The strong hand around her arm squeezed tighter.

"Cheerful, my ass! Just because the Yankees are here, you think you're gonna be free soon!"

"No, Massa George!" George Devon's hand gripped her arm so tightly she felt a sharp pain. "Please, sir! You're hurting me!"

"I'm gonna hurt you a lot more if you ever try to run from me!"

A delicate voice floated into the dining room. "Massa George? Something wrong, Massa?" Martha, Devonfield's housekeeper, entered the room. She was a tall, willowy woman with exquisite features on her creamy brown face.

The master's expression softened. He released June's arm. The young maid tossed Martha a grateful look and scurried away.

June stepped outside onto the veranda and inhaled the cold, crisp air. *Drunken bastard!* she thought bitterly, massaging her arm. She did not know how much longer she could put up with the likes of him. Perhaps she should leave. *And go where?* June wondered. *To the Yankees?*

Restlessly she paced around the porch. June was sixteen years old, stood at five feet five inches tall, and was blessed (cursed in her opinion) with a curvaceous figure. Her full lips, slanting brown eyes, and rich brown skin also attracted the attention of men.

George Devon had built up an enormous debt by 1858. To pay it off, the master initiated what Devonfield's slaves still called "the Big Sale." At least thirty had been sold to a Memphis dealer—among them June's parents and sister. Alone and frightened, June could not forgive him for separating her from her family.

Fortunately, there had been Martha to help the lonely twelve-year-old. Kindhearted Martha, who was also the master's mistress. What the housekeeper saw in George Devon eluded June. Contrary to most master-and-slave relationships, Martha had not been *forced* into Devon's bed. What did she see in that drunk?

"Hey, June! Where are you, girl?" A masculine voice cried out. "Aunt Sadie's got our Christmas breakfast ready!"

A tall, good-looking brown man with a ready smile strode around the corner of the three-story farmhouse. Even dressed in second-hand clothes, Harlin was something to look at. The former field hand, now footman, was very popular with the female slaves.

Strangely enough, June had never become one of his conquests. She had not been attracted to him romantically. Although June found him handsome, he possessed a hard streak in his mental makeup that prevented her from considering him as a beau. Instead the two had become good friends, partly because Harlin's two older brothers had also been part of the sale four years ago. Sharing and understanding each other's sorrow and loneliness had drawn the two adolescents into a close friendship.

"There you are, gal. Why didn't you answer back?" Harlin noticed her rubbing her forearm. "What happened?"

"Massa George's drunk again," June muttered.

Harlin nodded. Everyone was aware of George Devon's drunken bouts. They had started right after the Big Sale. The outbreak of war, the young master's death at Bull Run, Mistress Kate's suicide after news of young Johnny reached the plantation, and the disappearance of ten slaves last fall steadily increased George Devon's indulgence.

June continued. "All I said was 'Merry Christmas,' and he nearly broke my arm."

"Maybe it was the way you said it. Like you was expecting the Yanks to show up."

"Well shoot! I can't help it if they're around! Considering the way the war's been going, did he expect things to stay the same?" Everyone had heard rumors of General Rosecrans's Union army in the neighborhood. "Whether the Yanks show up or not, I ain't staying here forever!"

Harlin gave June a reassuring pat and guided her to the slave quarters. Long tables stood near the dilapidated cabins, with the Devonfield slaves surrounding them.

Christmas was the one day the slaves ate well. The tables groaned with ham, gravy, scrambled eggs, biscuits, fried potatoes, grits, and hoecakes. And this was just breakfast.

Both Harlin and June filled their tin plates with food and began to eat. June started to serve herself a second helping when a buggy carrying Master George and Martha appeared. The overseer, Bob Finney, rode beside them on his horse. The slaves halted their festivities and respectfully turned to look at their master.

"Morning all, and Merry Christmas!" Devon greeted. Except for a glassy look that remained in his eyes, he appeared more sober than a short while before.

The slaves, all except June, replied, "Morning, Massa George!" She merely eyed her master resentfully.

"I'm glad to see y'all enjoying your Christmas breakfast. Yes sir, it's good to see you bucks and wenches having a good time."

June rolled her eyes. Everyone knew they owed their breakfast to Martha and Finney. Devon was usually too drunk to know what was going on.

"I realize that you've heard rumors about the Yankees being in the neighborhood. Well, it's true. Be careful if you see them. These are dangerous bastards and they'll put you in camps, force you to work, starve you, or beat you if they can. Y'all be much happier staying here at Devonfield."

June saw Harlin hide the sneer on his face. Like him, she doubted she would be happier at Devonfield. The plantation was a prison, pure and simple. Not only did she dread having to go near Mr. Devon, she was not treated very well by the other slaves.

Because her family had been house slaves for as long as anyone could remember, Devonfield's other bondsmen regarded June with envy. "Too uppity," they had whispered behind her back. Perhaps she was. Deep down, June felt there was more to her than just being a slave. She refused to hide her feelings from the others, except Mr. Devon and Mr. Finney. And she was well-known among the plantation's slaves for her vicious temper. This caused the others to dislike her even more.

"Now y'all have a good eat," Devon continued,

"but not too much. You still have supper. Enjoy yourselves and Merry Christmas."

"Merry Christmas! Merry Christmas, Massa
George!" the slaves cried in unison. June remained
silent.

"Boy, that's the biggest pile of horseshit I've ever
heard!" Harlin declared, once the master was out of
earshot.

June asked Harlin why he hadn't already packed up
and left if he felt that way.

"June, honey, where there's Yanks, there's bound to
be Rebs. And I damn sure don't feel like walking into
the middle of some battle."

It was the same reason that had kept June at
Devonfield. With Rosecrans's Yanks and Bragg's
Confederates roaming about, it was not safe for a lone
slave girl to be roaming the countryside. Besides, she
had heard rumors that the white Yankees treated
blacks no better than the Rebs did.

As Harlin predicted, the fighting began six days
later, on the day of Devonfield's annual New Year's
Eve party. White guests from around the neighborhood appeared for the day-long festivities.

The party was in full swing by late afternoon when
the rumblings of cannonfire shook the drawing-room
walls. One female guest began to panic.

"Nothing to worry about, folks!" Mr. Devon
declared. "That's just General Bragg licking the Yanks
at Stone River!"

Everyone began to murmur at once. June did not
know whether any of them believed what the master

was telling them. The way Devon was swilling the punch, she wondered if even he believed his own words.

The battle raged on until late night. A few hours after the new year of 1863 was ushered in, Devonfield received news of the outcome.

"We licked 'em!" Finney cried, rushing into the drawing room with muddy boots. "Bragg has beaten back the Yankees north of Stone River!"

Cries of exhilaration from the guests filled the room. June's heart sank. What in the hell was wrong with those Yanks? They had been doing so well since Shiloh. June had expected to be freed within a few days. Now, with the Yankees retreating, she had lost her chance for an easy trip behind Union lines.

While the guests continued to celebrate, June went to the refreshment table, where Harlin was placing glasses of punch on a tray. "Did you hear?" she whispered.

"Yeah. I had hoped the Yanks would win. I reckon getting out of here is going to be harder now. There's still Yankees in Memphis and I've always wanted to see Nashville, so I'm leaving anyway." Harlin glanced at her. "You want to join me?"

June almost said no. Why, she did not know. After all, Harlin was her best friend. When she and the former field hand had first become close, many had warned her about him. "That boy's got a mean streak in him," Aunt Sadie had whispered. "Just like his mama. Massa George didn't sell her down the river for nothing!" Everybody knew the stories about

13

Harlin's mother offering herself to the former over-seer for favors. Many had believed her to be a thief who had taught Harlin and his brothers the tricks of the trade.

June merely dismissed the rumors. Other than Martha, Harlin had been the only true friend in her life since the loss of her family. Overcoming her hesitancy, she begged Harlin to wait until both armies had left the area. Then she would leave with him.

"All right, but I'm leaving in a week, no matter what."

They didn't have a week. The fighting on New Year's Eve turned out to be the first day of the Battle of Murfreesboro. The two armies took a respite on New Year's and resumed fighting the following day. This time, the Union emerged victorious. Two days later, Yankee cavalry appeared at Devonfield.

A drunken George Devon emerged on the veranda, brandishing a revolver. June, Martha, and Finney were right behind him.

A stocky man in uniform with small blue eyes and luxuriant side-whiskers dismounted. "Captain Erasmus Stirling of the 17th Indiana Cavalry at your service, sir. Are you George Devon of Devonfield?"

"Yeah!" Devon slurred. "What do you Yankee bastards want?"

Stirling's blue eyes froze. "May I suggest you control your tongue, sir? This is now Union territory."

"To hell with you, sir! I'll talk to you in any manner I please." Devon turned to Finney. "Bob! Get this pile of Yankee shit off my land!"

The lanky overseer hesitated. He shifted his gaze uneasily between his employer and the many horsemen behind Stirling. "But sir...," he began.

"Goddamit! Do as I say!"

The overseer took a step forward and someone fired a shot at him, narrowly missing his right foot. A grinning trooper in a sergeant's uniform held a smoking gun.

"Thank you, Sergeant Hatchett," Captain Stirling said. "Now, if you please sir, have your slaves turn over all livestock and grain available to...."

"Over my dead body!" Devon aimed his revolver at the officer.

Someone else fired a gun, and a bullet hole appeared between George Devon's eyes. June's master fell dead.

Shocked by the sudden violence, June stood immobilized as she stared at the lifeless body that was once her owner.

Martha let out a wail and fell upon Devon's body. "Oh, my Lord! Look what you've done, you bastards!" she cried. "You've killed him! That gun wasn't even loaded!"

No one bothered the grieving housekeeper. Stirling, the sergeant, and a few other troopers strode past her to enter the house, without even a glance her way.

June tried without success to pry Martha away from Devon's corpse. She turned to the overseer for assistance. "Mr. Bob," she said, "please, help me get Martha inside."

Finney, who had stood by like a scared rabbit,

shook himself out of his trance and helped June. They managed to get the housekeeper inside and into the library.

"You, sir." Captain Stirling appeared at the door. His eyes drilled into Finney's. "I need you to help us with the foraging. Are you willing to cooperate or do you want to end up like your employer?"

Finney's head hung low with defeat as he guided the captain toward the barn and stables.

It took the company all morning and afternoon to ransack Devonfield. June watched from the library window as blue-clad soldiers carried away pigs, turkeys, chickens, horses, sacks of grain, and one of the plantation's cows. She doubted if they had left anything for the plantation's inhabitants to survive.

Tired of watching the looting, June left Martha in the library and came across two soldiers out in the hall, carrying more booty. One of them, Sergeant Hatchett, had the family silver in his arms.

"Jesus!" she muttered before she could hold her tongue. The two men glanced at her sharply.

"What do you want, girl?" the sergeant asked. He spoke in a low, raspy voice.

June took a step backward toward the library, her eyes wide with fear. "Nothing. You and the Yank there took me by...."

"What are you doing?" Martha's loud voice rang through the hall from behind June. "That doesn't belong to you! Put it back!"

"You mind your business, wench!"

16

"*Put it back!*" Before June could stop her, Martha leaped upon the sergeant, causing him to drop the silver service. The two were soon on the floor, struggling.

The other Yank, a lanky redhead with a missing tooth, dumped his goods into a chair and started to pull his gun. June reacted faster. She grabbed hold of a vase from a table outside the library and swung it down upon the trooper's head.

The man cried out in pain, blood trickling down his hairline as he slumped to the floor.

As June moved away, she bumped into another man in blue uniform. The straps on the uniform's shoulder identified him as an officer. Looking into his fae, June realized it was the company captain.

"What the devil's going on?" Captain Stirling demanded. Finney was right behind him. "My God! Sergeant Hatchett! Get off that woman now! And get that private out of here!"

Red-faced, Sergeant Hatchett obeyed the captain. June helped Martha to her feet. Sobbing, the housekeeper clung to June. The captain continued, "Finney! I want the slaves out front! You, girl!" He directed these last words to June. "Get that woman upstairs!"

June escorted Martha to her room. A half hour later, June was back downstairs. She spotted the rest of Devonfield's twenty-five remaining slaves on the grounds in front of the house. The captain and another officer stood on the veranda facing them. June strode past the two men and joined the slaves.

"I assume all of you have heard of President

Lincoln's Emancipation Proclamation," Stirling began. He removed his yellow gloves and began slapping them against his left palm. The slaves stared at him with blank expressions.

Aunt Sadie spoke up. "I've heard rumors, sir. I once heard Massa George and Mister Bob talking about it."

"Well, this document frees all the slaves in the South except in border states—like Kentucky and Maryland." According to the Captain, those were slave states that remained in the Union. It made no sense to June. Why bother freeing slaves only under Rebel control? So much for Yankee freedom, she thought with contempt.

The captain continued. "But since this is now Union territory, and since there is no legal act that makes you totally free, you are all now wards of the United States. That means you're contraband. And the Army wants you to stay here and grow cotton for the Union."

The Union and who else?

"Can we leave?" Harlin asked.

"Uh, yes, but I wouldn't advise it. It would be much safer for you to remain here. We can take better care of you."

June thought, like hell I'm staying here! The farther away from Devonfield, the better for me. She glanced at Harlin. His eyes reflected the same thought.

"That's all." Stirling dismissed everyone and the slaves dispersed.

Harlin whispered in her ear. "I'm getting out tonight. I reckon there's a better way to earn money than picking cotton. How about it?"

June nodded.

"Good. Meet me behind the barn tomorrow morning."

Because she was a house slave and therefore subject to being called upon night and day, June had a room in the main house, a small, cramped space in the attic. Early the next morning, she was in her room stuffing her few belongings inside a gunnysack.

Quietly, she made her way down to the second floor. Martha's room was there and June wanted to say good-bye to the housekeeper. She leaned an ear close to the door to Martha's room. Not a peep. The housekeeper was probably asleep.

June opened the door and crept toward the bed. As she leaned forward to place a hand on Martha's shoulder, June froze with shock.

The housekeeper's face was masklike. Still. Yet there was blood congealed around her left wrist. Damp red stains soaked the bed. Martha had slit her wrist and bled to death. Tears fell down June's cheeks. Damn those Yanks and Master George! Poor Martha's life had been shot down on the veranda this morning. The housekeeper obviously could not bear the thought of a future without Mr. Devon.

Choking back her sobs, June turned away and left the house as quickly as she could.

"There you are, gal," Harlin said when she met him next to the barn. "I was beginning to wonder what was taking you so long."

It was cold. The shawl around June's neck wasn't enough to prevent the chill of the January dawn from seeping into her bones.

"Martha's dead."

"Huh?"

"Martha's dead. She cut her wrists." Tears still fell down June's cheeks.

"Jesus! I'm sorry, Juney gal."

June glanced at him sharply. Despite the words of pity, she detected a lack of concern in his tone. She felt angry. "Yeah, sure you are," June muttered under her breath.

They started to walk, but then something slipped from under Harlin's coat and hit the cold ground.

"What…?" June began. She picked up a piece of cloth filled with several gold coins. "Where did you get this?"

"From the library. It was inside the massa's desk."

"Harlin! You stole it! Not that I give a fig about Massa George, but he probably meant for Martha to have it!"

"Martha can't put it to use no more. She's dead. Remember?" Harlin grabbed her hand.

"How can you say something like that about her? She was like a sister to me! Don't you have any feelings?"

"Why should I care about some woman who was the massa's whore? I don't recall her doing anything for me!"

His cold-blooded attitude infuriated June. She stood there and glared at him. She had a good mind to go her own way.

Harlin tugged her hand. "Dammit, June! We don't

have all day! I can't help it if Martha and I never liked each other! Hell, I doubt she would cry any tears over my death. Now are you coming or not?"

June sighed. There was nothing else to do but go with him. Harlin was right. Martha had never thought much of him. Besides, he was all that she had now. She dismissed the negative thoughts from her mind and followed him into the night.

Chapter 2

Atchison, Kansas, April 1864.

"Where you two young folks headed?" a grizzled black man asked. Bits of gray sprinkled his thick, dark hair. He wore a blue calico shirt with trousers made from hide. A string of beads hung around his neck. A pipe was clenched between his teeth.

June opened her mouth to reply, but Harlin interrupted. He fixed the older man with a glare and said, "None of your damn business, nigger!"

"Nigger?" The man looked affronted. "Don't you be calling me nigger, boy! I don't take that from no one. Black or white."

Harlin made threatening steps toward the man, but the dangerous glint in the old man's eyes halted him in his tracks.

June decided things were getting out of hand, so

she stepped forward to ease the tensions and replied, "We don't know yet. We just came from Tennessee."

"Tennessee! That's a hell of a long way!"

It had been a long way indeed. June and Harlin had intended to head north for Chicago or Toronto. However, after overhearing two main deck passengers mention a gold rush in the Nevada Territory, they had changed their minds. That is, Harlin changed his mind and tried to convince June that their fortunes lay west. She had expressed doubts about the long trip and the danger of Indians. Yet she was unable to resist Harlin's smooth tongue. By the time their steamboat reached Nashville, June was convinced. There they found themselves in the employ of the Union army. With June working as a laundress and Harlin as a laborer, they followed the Army of the Cumberland from Nashville to Chattanooga by the fall of 1863.

In their different ways, the two friends developed a healthy dislike of the army. June especially resented the officers' arrogance, the strict regimentation of the work, and the brutal manner in which both officers and enlisted men treated the black workers. Ironically, Harlin turned out to be the deciding factor in their decision to leave.

Three months after the Battle of Chattanooga, an officer's wallet had turned up missing. All contraband working for the army were immediately suspected. Although a thorough search was made, the wallet had not been found. Two days later, Harlin suggested to June that they leave. June discovered why. It was Harlin who had stolen the wallet.

June tried to persuade him to return it, but Harlin refused. "I ain't gonna have my back marked up by a whip again." So the pair waited until the furor died down and slipped aboard a Tennessee River steamboat headed for the Ohio.

With the money Harlin had stolen, they felt sure they had enough to reach Virginia City. But Harlin's one-night bout of gambling in St. Louis caused their funds to dwindle severely. June had been furious. The two friends argued that night, even exchanging blows. Harlin slapped June, and she punched him back. The argument ended with the two barely on speaking terms.

June eventually forgave Harlin and loaned him some money for steamboat passage up the Missouri River. With the wages they had earned working for the army and the money Harlin had stolen, they now had eighty-nine dollars between them. June had no idea how far west they could go on those funds.

"We were heading for Virginia City but…," June threw a quick glance at Harlin, "I don't think we have enough to go all the way." She, Harlin, and their new acquaintance stood near some horses on the cargo deck.

Slowly, the steamboat eased toward the river levee.

"Virginia City, huh? The town's not much, but the country around it is beautiful. The name's Levi Walker." The man stuck out his hand. "Former mountain man, Santa Fe trader, and now rancher. I've got me a spread near the Sweetwater in Wyoming Territory."

June shook Levi's hand. "June Daley." Her new surname was an Anglicized version of Dele, the name of her father's African ancestor. Unbeknownst to their masters, June's family had always used it.

Levi replied, "Nice to meet you. I won't ask who your friend is. I reckon he don't want me to know."

Harlin scowled and looked away.

"If you two are continuing west, I'd keep a sharp eye out for bushwhackers in Kansas. We were lucky to get through Missouri. The guerrillas on both sides, especially Rebs, have been attacking steamboats on this river. Kansas'll be worse."

"Does it matter since we're going farther west?" June asked.

"You'll need to keep yourselves sharp out there. The army and white settlers are stirring up trouble with some tribes. 'Specially the Cheyenne, Arapaho, and Sioux. For years the whites been trespassing on their land. They're finally showing how they feel about it."

"How do you know?"

"My wife's Cheyenne. I've been living out west for over thirty years."

"Thanks. We'll do as you say." *Decent man*, she thought. She noticed that the boarding ramp had been lowered. "I guess we be leaving now."

"Take care of yourself." Levi gave her one last smile as she and Harlin disembarked. They merged into the crowd on the levee, which was made up of people from wagon trains, emigrants, and the military.

"Did you hear that?" she asked Harlin.

Harlin snorted. "Yeah, I heard. That old man just whistling in the wind." He made another sound and muttered, "Mountain man, my foot."

"Didn't you see what he was wearing? Those buckskin trousers of his? He's one of those wilderness men—just like Davy Crockett and Daniel Boone. He's even got an Indian wife."

"So what?"

June said nothing. Harlin had certainly been in a foul mood lately. Especially since their fight in St. Louis.

The ticket vendor at the Overland Express booth told them that the next stage west would depart the following day around noon. "How much money you have?"

Harlin told him.

"Well, that's enough for two tickets to Denver, with six dollars left over," the vendor said.

Denver. June and Harlin glanced at each other. It wasn't Nevada, but it was better than being stuck in Kansas. Since Colorado was in the midst of its own gold rush, there would be plenty of jobs available. All they needed was extra money for two tickets to Virginia City, and they should be able to earn that easily.

"If you're looking for a room here in town," the vendor continued, "there's a place called Black Delia's Hotel. It's the only hotel in town that takes colored folks."

Harlin thanked the vendor and purchased two tickets for Denver. They found Black Delia's Hotel on the northern end of Main Street. It was a two-story boardinghouse run by a former slave from Virginia. The pair spent twenty minutes trying to convince the plump proprietor that they were brother and sister so they could get a room together. There was not enough of their money left for two rooms.

Later that evening, June and Harlin entered the crowded dining room for their meal. Not many whites boarded at Black Delia's, but the owner's southern-style cooking attracted many during suppertime.

The two friends finally found empty seats at a table and became acquainted with a man who was also waiting for the westbound stage. "My name's Charlie Taylor," he said. The man was slender and broad-shouldered, with hazel-brown eyes, cocoa-brown skin, and thin features. June found him very handsome, especially in the blue uniform he was wearing.

June introduced Harlin and herself. "How long have you been in the army?" she asked.

"Two years. I joined up with Jim Lane, the abolitionist. The First Kansas Volunteers."

Born in Missouri as a slave, Charlie and his family had been freed by a master who had become disenchanted with the "peculiar institution." That had happened ten years ago when Charlie was twelve. Instead of remaining with their former master, the Taylors decided to move to the free territory of Nebraska.

"My daddy owns a farm outside Rock Creek."

June asked, "Is that where you going?"

"No. I'm reporting back for duty. I was on a furlough. Break." Charlie eagerly turned toward Harlin. "By the way, the army's accepting colored men. If you want to fight, you best join up now before the war's over."

Harlin greeted Charlie's advice with derision, replying with a sneer, "Do you take me as some kind of fool? What in the hell makes you think I want to join the army? I had enough of those bastards back in Tennessee."

Although she agreed with Harlin, June kept her thoughts to herself. She realized Charlie was just trying to be friendly and didn't deserve Harlin's open scorn.

Since St. Louis, June had been considering following her first instincts and leaving Harlin. But she couldn't. The two had been through too much together and she couldn't allow a few bad moments to break up a friendship. She eyed the corporal's handsome brown face with interest. There was no reason, however, to allow Harlin to prevent her from making new friends.

The three caught the westbound stagecoach the next morning. The driver would not allow those of color to sit inside the coach. So June, Harlin, and Charlie were forced to bounce on the seats situated above the driver's.

To June, the grassy plains of Kansas were a contrast to the wooded country they had just left. She loved it. Although not as green as back east, the open, vast country had its own special beauty. The blue sky and the rolling plains seemed to go on forever in parallel lines. For the first time, June felt completely free.

A day after leaving Atchison, the stagecoach arrived at Fort Hays. The two friends bid the departing soldier good-bye. At least June did. Harlin merely nodded and turned his attention away from Charlie.

"Can I have one word with you before the stage leaves, Miss June?" Charlie asked. He steered June away from the coach. "I reckon I have no cause to speak like this, but if I were you, I'd keep an eye on your friend. I like you a lot and I'd hate to see anything happen to you."

For a moment June was annoyed by Charlie's presumptuous remark. Then memories from the past came back. Harlin's thefts, his behavior in St. Louis and on this trip, and his rudeness toward Levi Walker and Charlie. She almost considered the trooper's advice, but then decided against it. Harlin was just going through a bad mood.

She shook his hand and smiled. "Don't worry. I'm sure I'll be fine. Thanks for thinking of me." June kissed his right cheek. "Bye." As the stage rolled away from the fort, she noticed the red flush on Charlie's cheek and was pleased. Not a bad fellow. A little finicky at times but not bad. And damned good-looking too.

Denver resembled a city under siege when June and Harlin finally arrived on a morning in early May. Men everywhere toted guns. The fear on the faces of the people was unmistakable. June recalled Levi Walker's remarks on the territory's troubles with the Cheyenne and Arapaho.

"Well damn! I'm surprised you made it in, Beau!" cried an employee of the stage line as the coach pulled into the station. "Surprised but glad." He was a thin rail of a man with round spectacles.

The driver put the brakes on and jumped from his seat. "Why? Has there been trouble?"

As they stepped down from the coach, June and Harlin overheard the thin employee describe an Indian attack on a settlement. "Those savage bastards burned the Marstons' place on the South Platte four days ago. The whole family was found dead and scalped."

June was glad to be in Denver and not on the road to Nevada. With so much bloodshed on the plains, there was a chance she could find herself in the way of a bullet or an arrow. She had always sympathized with the Indians over being pushed off their lands. One of her grandmothers had been part Cherokee. But in this instance, preservation of her own skin came first.

The Pike's Peak Gold Rush of 1858–1859 had brought in an influx of gold seekers and settlers to this territory, much to the dismay of its original occupants. In a matter of six years, whites had poured into hunting grounds, scattered the buffalo, and pushed, wheedled, or killed Cheyenne and Arapaho to grab the land for themselves. Unable to tolerate the situation, the tribes were now retaliating.

Although Denver's somewhat ramshackle appearance was not what June had expected, many people filled its streets and business seemed thriving.

"Shouldn't be too hard to find a good job in this place," Harlin commented as they strode down Fourteenth Street. "Look at 'em. Everyone's living high off the hog! I bet we will be soon. Just gotta find the right job."

There were many jobs offered all right. Menial ones. Wherever the two went, they were offered positions waiting tables, cleaning homes, stables, or spittoons, washing dishes or clothes, and cooking. June would have gladly accepted one just to earn the money they needed. But Harlin wanted something better. Unfortunately for him, they had yet to meet someone who was willing to offer two Negroes less menial jobs.

"Let's try a saloon," Harlin suggested after they left a restaurant on Blake Street. It was owned by a black man named Barney Ford, and Harlin declared he had no intention of working for a "nigger."

An hour later, they came across their fifth saloon, a large building on Thirteenth Street. Above the door hung an ornate sign—"The Southern Cross Saloon." Right next door was another building, a two-story frame house with lace curtains and no sign attached to it. Probably the saloon owner's private home.

"Juney! Over here!" Harlin pointed to a bulletin board outside the swinging doors of the saloon. "What does that say?" While working as a laundress, June had learned how to read and write.

She peered at the handbill. "'Jobs av-ai-lable at the Southern Cross Saloon. Short hours, good pay. See

Allen Cross.' I reckon there's jobs available here."

"I think we've found our place."

"Sorry, boy, spittoon cleaner is all I got to offer," declared a tall, muscular man with a neatly trimmed beard and elegant clothes. He sat himself down in a chair behind a mahogany desk and lit up a cigar.

The two friends were in the private office of the saloon's owner. The Southern Cross was unlike anything June had ever seen. She had never been inside a saloon before, and the old homes of Tennessee did not have such colorful and gaudy ornamentation. Scarlet red kerosene lamps, wide mirrors, a long, polished bar of mahogany, gaming tables, a large painting of a woman with no clothes, and to the left of the door, a platform where shapely women dressed in bright blue corselets, black stockings, and high heels kicked up their legs to the music of a piano player.

June and Harlin had to go upstairs to reach Cross's private office. The saloon owner paid much attention to the sheaf of papers in his hands.

His dark eyes made a sudden quick appraisal of June's full-figured body. Somehow she felt exposed.

"Course," he continued, "I can offer this wench here a better paying job. It would require less costume."

Revulsion crept up June's spine as she understood what he meant. She had no intention of offering her body for sale. Might as well be some damn slave concubine on a plantation! Having herself cut up and fed to the hunting dogs was preferable.

June replied tersely, "No thanks. Not to my tastes."

"I charge ten dollars per customer. We're very expensive here. You get to keep twenty-five percent of the night's profits." He turned to Harlin. "And I might just let you stay on as a guard for this place."

Harlin started to open his mouth. "*No thank you!*" June insisted. "I ain't gonna earn my living humping twenty men a night!"

The saloon owner shrugged and brushed his fawn-colored jacket lightly. "Fine. Suit yourself. You can leave the way you came."

It was a dismissal that June did not need to hear twice. She was eager to leave anyhow. Once the two friends were back outside, June cried out, "Can you believe that man? Thinking I'd be desperate enough to take a job like that? Hell, I'd rather be back at Devonfield."

Harlin, she noticed, seemed distracted. He hardly said a word.

"Harlin?"

"Hmmmm?"

"What is it? You thinking I should have taken that job?"

"Of course not! What do you take me for?" He paused momentarily and sighed. "Well, Juney gal, looks like it's gonna take us awhile longer to get to Virginia City. Maybe we should go back to that hotel after all."

The two returned to the restaurant they had stopped at before searching the saloons. The handsome black man immediately hired June as a maid and Harlin as a handyman. The pair also found room and board at a boardinghouse just two blocks away.

After completing their first day of work, they washed up and joined their fellow boarders for supper, then went upstairs to their rooms. Tired from the strenuous day, June immediately prepared for bed after her meal. While she was brushing her hair, Harlin came by her room to say good night. She noticed that he was wearing his best clothes.

"Where are you going?" she asked.

"Out. Thought I'd check out the town's evening entertainment."

"Have fun. And don't get into any trouble."

Harlin turned to her with a devil-may-care smile on his face. Lord, was that man handsome! "Now Juney, you know me better than that."

"Don't I just!"

Harlin laughed heartily and waved good-bye He was out of her room before she had time to say more.

Sleep came as a blessed event. It was the first decent rest June had experienced since Atchison. A few hours later, she was roused by the sound of footsteps outside her room. Harlin must have returned for the night, she figured. June closed her eyes again and went back to sleep.

The next thing she knew, rough hands jerked her from the bed and stuffed a piece of cloth in her mouth so that she could not cry out. She struggled fiercely until someone forced a rough burlap sack over her head. Then she was trussed up like a Christmas turkey and slung over a shoulder.

Harlin! Her mind cried. She hoped and prayed that he would arrive and rescue her. She could not imagine what was going on. Why would someone try to abduct her in this manner? She hardly even knew anyone in Denver.

Carried downstairs and dumped unceremoniously into a wagon, June ignored her bruised body as she desperately tried to tear the sack off her head. But bound up as she was, it was impossible. To make matters worse, she was having difficulty breathing. The harder she struggled, the thinner the air became until she completely blacked out.

A brown blur appeared before June's eyes. The blur eventually became a face. It was a full, plump brown face with sad brown eyes.

June rubbed her eyes. "Where am I?" she croaked.

The face answered, "Mr. Allen and Miz Therese's place."

"Mr. Allen?"

"Allen Cross. This here's the Southern Cross."

Of course. The name conjured up memories of an opulent saloon and a well-dressed white man who had coolly dismissed her and Harlin. The saloonkeeper must have kidnapped her. June uttered what sounded like a moan.

"You all right, honey?" the woman asked.

"That bastard," June hissed. She swallowed hard. Her throat was dry.

The plump woman handed her a tin cup of water.

June drank it all within seconds. "My name's Thelma. I'm the housekeeper here. Who was you calling a bastard? Mr. Allen? Or that friend of yours?"

"My friend? What do you mean?" June stared at Thelma.

The housekeeper revealed how Harlin had come to the saloon the previous evening. For five hundred dollars he had offered to deliver June to the saloon and Cross. "After you were left here, I saw Mr. Allen give him the money."

As she listened to the explanation and realized the implications of where she was and what was to be expected of her, June became blinded with rage and a loud roar filled her ears. Trying to restrain herself, June asked, "How do I know you're telling the truth?"

"Why would I lie?"

"Because your boss told you to. Or paid you. So I can blame Harlin."

"Honey, that friend of yours sold you. I reckon you can blame Mr. Allen as well. After all, he did buy you."

June realized Thelma was right. That lying, backstabbing bastard had betrayed her! Sold her for five hundred dollars! He should pray that money would get him away as far as possible.

From that moment on, June swore she would find Harlin if it took her the rest of her life. And if possible, make him pay dearly.

Chapter 3

Denver, Colorado Territory, May 1864.

The day after June regained consciousness at the Southern Cross Saloon, she stood in the center of her new bedroom, dressed in a chemise, pantalettes, and a corset. The crinoline hoopskirt fastened around her waist swayed about her legs. Thelma was helping her prepare for her first evening on the job.

June felt like a piece of meat being prepared for a banquet. And because she was unable to ignore this feeling, she resented the housekeeper's presence.

How could Thelma act as if June was going to a party? Didn't the woman realize what she was about to go through? If only the housekeeper would offer to help her get away! But no, it was obvious Thelma feared Allen Cross too much. June realized that the housekeeper could not be trusted.

"Mr. Allen says he wants me to make you look special tonight. Most girls who start here have to work in the saloon, walking about in their underthings. But Mr. Allen says he's gonna start you out in the parlor next door." The plump housekeeper slipped a rosy pink gown over the immobile June.

The gown fit perfectly. "There." Thelma stood back to survey the results. "You sure look good in that gown, girl. Sit down."

June was guided to the dresser and mirror and seated herself on the stool. Thelma started on her hair. By the time the older woman was finished, June's hair was elegantly coiffured with elaborate thick braids wrapped about her head.

A blank expression remained on June's face as she glanced at her reflection in the mirror. "Listen, honey," Thelma said. "No use crying over spilled milk. Might as well set your mind to it. It'll hurt a bit at first, but you'll get used to it."

"No, I won't," June replied stonily.

"Sure you will. Course, whether you like it or not is up to you. C'mon, the boss wants to see you."

The two made their way to Cross's office down the hall. It was different from the one above the saloon. June felt clumsy in the wide crinoline skirt. Thelma instructed her to take small steps. "That way your skirt won't sway and cause you to trip."

They entered Cross's office. Like the hallway, it was different from the one June had been in earlier with Harlin. And the saloonkeeper was not alone. A tall, statuesque woman with black hair and sharp features stood behind him.

Cross let out a low whistle as his dark eyes appraised June. "Well now! Don't you look special? Forget ten dollars. I think I'll charge twenty for you instead." He ordered her to take a seat. "Before I lay the rules, are you a virgin?"

"What?" The question shocked June.

"Are you a virgin? Dammit, girl! Has anyone taken you?"

June shook her head.

"Good. Then I'll charge your first customer an extra twenty dollars. First off, this is Madame Therese Aubry. She's my partner in the parlor. She'll lay down the rules for you." Cross turned to the tall woman. "*Cherie*?"

Pale green eyes met June's dark ones as Madame Aubry said, "Thelma will show you how to clean yourself after every customer. If you get pregnant, tell me or Monsieur Cross. We'll provide a doctor to get rid of it. No insults or harm to the customer unless it's in self-defense. No stealing. And...."

Cross interrupted. "And most importantly, no holding back cash from us. Like I said before, you'll get a twenty-five percent take of your evening's earnings." Cross's eyes took on a hard glitter as he continued. "You hold back any of your earnings, that pretty little face of yours won't look so good after I'm finished with you." He smiled coldly. June shivered.

"If you follow these rules," Therese Aubry continued, "no harm will come to you. We also don't allow any customer to hurt you. Anyone who does will get

41

the same treatment. Each customer is examined by a doctor before we allow him upstairs with a girl. Now, your first customer is waiting for you. Come."

The creole madam led June downstairs. The parlor was spacious and clean. Kerosene lamps lit the large room filled with plush chairs and settees. The pine walls were painted in canary yellow, and lace curtains hung in front of the windows. June recognized the curtains and realized she was in the frame house situated next door to the saloon.

There was nothing opulent about the decorations inside the parlor. But the sight of the women lounging about—some beautiful, some attractive, and others merely plain—took June by surprise. Although some were dressed in gowns like her, others were wearing only underclothes. Some were even topless!

One of the latter, a petite, brown-haired woman with delicate features, made her way toward the same man Therese was guiding June to. He was tall and blond with sparkling blue eyes. The topless prostitute reached him first.

"Hi, Tim honey! Been waiting for me?" she crooned, pressing herself against his body. June noticed that he did not seemed interested in her.

Therese gently brushed the topless whore aside. "Eugenie, *cherie*, why don't you find another customer. *Hein*?" Before Eugenie could protest, she brought June face-to-face with the customer. "Tim, this is our new girl, June. You said you wanted someone new. Well, here she is."

He was tall. Just over six feet and ruggedly built.

He looked at her with friendly eyes. "Hello. It's nice to meet you, June." He took her hand and shook it. "You're a very pretty girl."

"Thanks." It was the only word June uttered. She was too stunned by the realization that she was about to service her first man.

To make up for the lapse in conversation, Therese suggested that June and Tim go upstairs to her room. "I'll have a boy bring up some whiskey."

"No champagne, Therese?" Tim asked.

"Sorry, *cherie*. We haven't been able to get any since last fall."

"Oh well." Tim indicated the staircase with his hand. "Shall we go?" he said to June. She stared deeply into his eyes, dreading this moment. He took her by the arm and guided her toward the foot of the stairs. "Don't worry, sweetheart, I'll try not to hurt you."

It did hurt. At least it did when he breached her maidenhood. After that, he was very gentle with her. Both she and Tim managed to enjoy each other more vigorously the second time.

She learned a lot about her first customer. Timothy McPherson was part owner of a mine just north of the city. The other owner was his older brother.

"Nate and I came here from Ohio five years ago. We were among the lucky few to strike it rich in placer mines." He and June lay side by side. Her left breast pressed against his side, and he had one arm about her shoulder. "Nearly everyone else went bust."

43

"I heard the gold's all played out here."

"It's not all played out. We just have to dig a little deeper into the mountains. That's why Nate and I formed a mining company. We had another strike just two years ago. Course the troubles with the Arapaho and Cheyenne is making it hard for us to continue digging."

Tim sat up and poured a glass of whiskey from the bottle on the side table. "Would you like a glass?"

"No thanks," June replied. "I don't drink."

Tim looked at her. "I swear, you sure don't seem like the type of girl who'd be in a job like this. How did you get here anyway?"

June averted her eyes. "Ran out of money."

"So? Why not get a service job as a maid or cook?"

June sighed. She really didn't want to discuss the subject. And Tim's persistence to find out was ruining the good mood she had managed to achieve.

"Never mind," said Tim. "When you feel you can talk about it, I'm all ears." He finished his whiskey and set the glass on the table.

"My friend sold me to Mr. Cross."

"What?"

"My best friend sold me to this place for five hundred dollars." June proceeded to tell him about herself and how she had ended up in Denver. When she had finished, her voice was choked with tears she was struggling to hold back.

"There, there, honey," Tim muttered. He held her closer in his arms. "That's a fine thing for a friend to do to you. Hell, I don't know what to say."

After a few moments of silence, he added, "You know, come to think of it, if I were you, I'd put a bullet right between his eyes if I ever ran into him again."

June said nothing. Instead, she snuggled even closer to him. His advice sounded good to her.

Timothy McPherson became one of June's regular customers. Others include a merchant named Maxwell, two other miners, and an army colonel named Bertram St. John. Within three months, she was one of the top girls in the Southern Cross. Within five, she *was* the top.

Two particular whores resented June's meteoric rise. Eugenie Gault, the one who had tried to snatch Tim away that first night, was one. Before June's appearance, and ever since Cross and Aubry had owned their first cathouse in New Orleans, she had been the queen of the stable. What puzzled June was why Eugenie—or "Ginny," as she was called—circulated every night topless. Only the plain whores did that, the ones who couldn't catch customers with their faces alone.

"She likes to show her body," Clarice told June one blustery afternoon during the third week of November. The two of them were in the backyard taking down the wash. "That girl's been proud of her body ever since Evan had that large picture of her naked hanging in the house back in New Orleans."

Ginny, it seemed, was not prepared to be toppled from the throne by some dark-skinned novice. Nor was Lucy Webb, a beautiful mulatto from Louisville with a penchant for giggling. She was Ginny's greatest supporter and friend. "Ginny's faithful dog," was what Clarice called her.

June liked Clarice, although she had been reserved at first. The twenty-six-year-old woman had been a prostitute for eight years. Possessing a short, delicate frame, a pretty brown face, and wide, innocent brown eyes, Clarice Smith had led many of her customers to believe she had a sweet, childlike nature. However, underneath that innocent exterior was an intelligent mind, observing eyes, and a sharp tongue. June had taken to her at once.

"I noticed that," June replied to Clarice's dig at Lucy. "But how come she hangs out on the upstairs balcony in her drawers all day?"

"So she can be seen, girl! What else? That way the men passing by will see her and come looking for her at night. Like Ginny, she's really full of herself."

June discovered that both Ginny and Lucy were unpopular with the other whores. In the past, the two had been considered the top girls at the Southern Cross. The others were happy that June had managed to knock them out of their positions without developing a superior attitude of her own.

As the two friends continued to hang up clothes on the line, a pair of uniformed riders galloped by, nearly splattering mud on the clean laundry.

"Goddamn bluebellies!" Clarice cried angrily. "Can't they watch where they're going?"

June stared at the receding horseback figures down the street. "Looks like a lot of activity. I bet the army is planning a battle or something."

"A battle? I thought the army and the Indians had signed a peace treaty?"

Just two months before, a group of Cheyenne and Arapaho chiefs led by Black Kettle had ridden into Denver. They had met with the territorial governor to try to negotiate an end to the violence between the red men and the whites. As a concession to the army, Black Kettle had agreed to settle his people at a fort near Sand Creek in eastern Colorado.

June grunted. "Are you kidding? I suspect the folks here don't really want peace. What they want is to have every red man, woman, and child either dead or gone for good."

Events proved June correct. It was not long before the occupants in the frame house next to the saloon learned of the "battle" of Sand Creek. A colonel of the territorial militia, a former minister named John Chivington, led a surprise attack on Black Kettle's village.

The peaceful Cheyenne had not yet awakened when Chivington and his men swooped down and killed every Cheyenne they could lay their hands on. They did not discriminate over age or sex.

"How many Aprapaho and Cheyenne were out there?" asked one of the whores, a one-quarter Arapaho named Kitty. She and the other occupants sat around the breakfast table the day after the massacre. Thelma was frying eggs.

Therese scanned the newspaper in her hand. "Five hundred, I think." She puffed on the cigarette in her mouth. "It says here some of them managed to escape."

"They should have gone after them, if you ask me," Ginny commented, unable to hold her spiteful tongue. "Chivington did Denver a favor by getting rid of those red varmints."

Kitty's face paled suddenly and she rushed out of the kitchen.

"Nice going, Ginny," June said sharply. "You sure know how to stick your knife in the right spot."

Fried eggs hit June squarely in the face. "Mind your damn tongue, you half-assed nigger!" Ginny cried. "Nobody gave you call to speak to me like that!"

Lucy giggled.

June wiped the eggs away, grabbed the chestnut whore by the lapels of her robe, and forced her against the wall. Through clenched teeth June hissed, "Watch who you call 'nigger,' you little pasty-faced bitch! You call me that again, I'll cut your tongue out!"

Ginny trembled with fear while June maintained her grip on the lapels. Therese broke up the two. "Stop it! No fighting in here!"

June refused to release Ginny.

"June! Let her go! You know better than to fight! It's against the rules!"

Struggling to contain her emotions, June did as she was told and returned to her seat. One day, she and that uppity bitch were going to have it out.

All of Denver celebrated the victory at Sand Creek. Chivington was declared a savior and feted by the city's grateful citizens. June was glad to know that Tim wasn't one of them.

"My brother tried to get me to join the volunteers, but I couldn't make war on peaceful Indians. Hell, if there had been a war party, I'd have joined. But Black Kettle made it clear that he only wanted peace."

Another person who was disgusted by the affair was Kitty. So much so that she left the whorehouse by stealth two nights later.

"I reckon she went to find out if any of her kin were still alive," a blond-haired, blue-eyed whore told June the following afternoon. Leanne Simpkins, like Clarice and Ginny, was an old-timer from New Orleans, having been one of Cross and Therese's first girls. "She better hope and pray Jimmy don't find her. Mr. Allen paid two hundred dollars for her. A bought girl can't leave until she reimburses the money Mr. Allen paid for her."

June was aware of that. Cross and Therese had made it quite clear she could never leave their employ until she repaid the five hundred dollars given to Harlin, with a fifteen percent interest added. This was the standard rule for all girls sold into the house. June envied Kitty's escape, and she hoped that she succeeded.

Besides Kitty's disappearance (she was never caught), Sand Creek caused other consequences. Although warfare continued on the plains, Denver was no longer a besieged city. Adulation for John Chivington turned to disgust when actual details of the massacre were revealed.

Washington set up an army tribunal to investigate the incident. Although the court exonerated the colonel officially, the name John Chivington came to be reviled throughout the land ever afterward.

The whorehouse occupants went on with the normal routine of their lives. The quarrel that had flared between June and Ginny developed into a bitter feud, with most of the women siding with June.

One particular incident occurred one night in late April. After her first customer left, June discovered ground glass in her douche water. The moment the whorehouse closed its doors, June rushed immediately toward Ginny's room and found traces of glass on the whore's dresser. A violent tussle ensued, with most of the girls cheering June on. By the time Therese intervened, June had Ginny flat on the floor with her hands tight around Ginny's throat.

In the spring of 1865, the War Between the States ended with the surrender of the Confederate armies throughout the South. June found herself wondering if Devonfield was still standing. She recalled reading about the battles of Franklin and Nashville during the previous winter.

Word of the assassination of President Abraham Lincoln sent waves of shock and grief through the Denver citizens. Allen and Therese were two who did not share in the grief. Both had relatives in Louisiana. June was another. She felt sorry for the Lincoln family, but during her stint as an army laundress, she had heard a few hard-line abolitionists complain about the late President's delay in making slavery an issue of the war. She also remembered the complaints made by Charlie Taylor, the soldier she and Harlin had met in their travels, against the government's unfair policy of unequal pay for black soldiers.

Charlie Taylor. June remembered that he had warned her not to trust Harlin, and she hadn't bothered to listen. She was paying for her mistake now. Only memories of Harlin's betrayal—and her desire for revenge—kept June going. If she could endure another year in this place, she would have enough money to get out of the whorehouse with enough left over to resettle somewhere else, perhaps farther west.

Fall arrived again in Denver. In October, peace commissioners came to talk with the Cheyenne and Arapaho. The two tribes decided to lay down their arms and quietly move to designated reservations.

"Thank God!" one of June's regulars, Colonel St. John, declared. "Black Kettle and some of his band are heading south into the Indian Territory. That means no more killing." June and the officer lay side by side in bed after a heated bout between the sheets. For a straitlaced, simple man, St. John was very enjoyable in bed. June liked him.

"When the violence continued after Sand Creek, I wondered if another massacre would occur. It's funny but what I remembered most about Sand Creek was a pair of volunteers. I had spotted these two charmers selling Cheyenne scalps to theater owners and customers on the streets. Very unsavory. Of course, they didn't seem so at first. Good-looking fellows too. One colored, the other white. I hear they are now riding with Bert Todd."

Bert Todd was the territory's new scourge. He was an ex-jayhawker from Kansas who had turned to crime after the Indian threat had subsided. June's ears perked with interest when St. John mentioned the black man.

"Do you know who they are?"

"Ben Carlson and Harlin Mason."

June stiffened.

"Strange combination, a Hoosier and a Negro. Another one of Chivington's ex-volunteers recognized them from a description given by a passenger who had been on this stagecoach they had robbed. I think they're in Kansas now."

The officer continued talking but June did not hear him. Her mind raced with thoughts of Harlin, the son of a bitch! Hearing a report of his activities was almost like seeing him again. Rage swelled in her breast. That bastard had been in Denver while she had been languishing in this damn whorehouse! Selling Indian scalps on the street corners, huh? And robbing stagecoaches. That five hundred dollars must not have lasted very long.

After St. John left, June was in a dark mood. Downstairs in the parlor, she spotted Ginny on the settee, trying to seduce a customer.

"Just wait a moment lover, I'll be right back," Ginny crooned and left the befuddled man alone. The moment the whore walked away, June zeroed in on the customer. He didn't have a chance. In her aquamarine, low-cut gown, she was a striking figure—and much more desirable than a blowsy-looking Ginny in underwear and robe.

June and the customer were heading for the staircase when Ginny returned, carrying two glasses of champagne. "Hey! What the hell you think you're doing?"

"What does it look like?" June replied offhandedly. "If you leave a customer alone for one minute, he's fair game to the rest of us. You know the rule." She turned to the customer and said, "Come on, sugar." The blushing man followed her upstairs.

The next afternoon, June was outside, getting a breath of fresh air when Thelma appeared.

"June!" The round housekeeper ambled toward her. "Mr. Allen and Miz Therese wants to see you in the office."

A few minutes later, June entered the office on the second floor. Standing a few feet away from the two brothel keepers was Jimmy Morrow, the house bouncer. A warning bell rang inside June's head. Trouble was coming.

"You want to see me, Mr. Cross? Therese?"

Cross quietly examined the view outside the window. Therese, sitting at the desk, eyed June coldly. And the bouncer, a big hulk with blond hair and small blue eyes, repeatedly slammed his right knuckles into his left palm—smiling all the time.

Cross turned to her. His dark eyes resembled lumps of coal. "Yes, June, we did. Madame Aubry and I want you to explain this." He handed her a note.

It read:

Mr. Allen,
I saw June put some money under her mattress
last night. I think she's holding out on you.

It was unsigned.

"We want to know why you held back more than your share from last night. Jimmy found the fifty dollars under your mattress."

Speechless, June stared at Cross with a frozen expression. Her night's take was always put into a jar in her room and later deposited in the bank. *How had fifty dollars ended up under her mattress?*

"I..., I...," she stammered. June took a deep breath. "I didn't, Mr. Cross. I don't know how that money got there."

Therese snapped at her, "Don't lie! You've been stealing our money! We caught you red-handed. How long have you been stealing from us?"

"I swear to God! I don't know! I don't even put my take there! I usually put it in a jar!"

"Liar!" The madam turned to Cross. "I think it's time we used more extreme methods."

Sighing, Cross shook his head. "June, June, June. In nearly two years, you've managed to become our top girl. And now you want to ruin it all with this? How disappointing." He nodded at the bouncer. "OK, Jimmy, I think a slap first."

The hulk moved slowly toward June. Desperately, she glanced around the room for an avenue of escape.

Jimmy had the doorway blocked. Before she could move, June felt a stinging blow across her cheek. She fell back with a gasp.

Cross said, "Now, shall we start again?"

Chapter 4

Denver, Colorado Territory, Winter 1865–66.

Jimmy grabbed hold of June's forearm and slapped her again. Harder.

"I don't want to be here all afternoon, girl," Cross said as he glanced at his pocketwatch.

June pleaded. "Mr. Cross, I swear to God I don't know how that money got there! Please!" *Jesus!* She had not groveled like this since Devonfield. It was like the return of an old nightmare. Only instead of a whip, she was threatened with fists.

The bouncer raised his hand again.

"No!" June cried. She turned to the cold-eyed madam. "Therese! Didn't you check my box? You know how many customers I had last night. If you check, the right amount will be there!"

Each girl kept a cast-iron box with her name on it

in the small waiting room across the hall from the front parlor. After bidding a customer good-bye, she was to put the cash into the box. After the whorehouse closed for the night, Therese and Allen would collect the money, count it, and the next morning distribute to each girl her share.

The two owners looked at each other. Therese nodded. "That doesn't mean anything. Perhaps this fifty dollars was a tip."

"Why don't you ask my customers? I had three of them last night—Mr. Maxwell, some miner named McCook, and a Mr. Dan Preston, who runs a harness shop down the street."

"Jimmy, go check them out," Cross ordered. The bouncer seemed disappointed by the aborted beating. He left and June was kept in her room with the door locked.

An extremely tense two hours passed before Jimmy returned. June was summoned again.

"She's telling the truth, Mr. Cross," Jimmy told them. "They each paid her twenty-five dollars."

Therese looked contrite as she turned to June. "Sorry you had to go through that, *cherie*. Please understand that we had to know. After all, business is business."

Relief flooded over June.

"June," Cross said, "whoever set you up is gonna answer to me. I promise. You don't even have to work tomorrow."

"Thank you, Mr. Cross, Miss Therese," June replied

quietly. She did not say anything further. Instead she left the office as quickly as she could. God help the person who had framed her. And if it was the person June suspected, she hoped perhaps the Lord might not bother to lend a helping hand.

Later that afternoon, June was about to enter the kitchen to get something to eat when she overheard a voice—Lucy's. "You put fifty dollars under her bed to make Mr. Allen think she was holding back?" she squealed.

Ginny protested. "Not so loud! You want everyone to hear you?"

June peeked inside. The two friends sat at the kitchen table, sipping coffee. Ginny took a flask from the pocket of her robe and poured the contents into her cup. June remained in the hall.

"I even left a note with Therese to make sure they would look," Ginny continued.

"Well, whatever you did didn't work."

The chestnut-haired whore flashed her friend a dark look. "What do you mean?" she asked sharply.

"I saw Jimmy leave. I think he went to check with her customers. And I just saw her go to her room not long ago. Her face didn't hardly looked messed up at all."

"Damn! I didn't think they would bother checking with her men."

"Why did you set her up?"

"That bitch thinks she's the best thing around here. I just wanted her to know she's in the same boat as the rest of us."

June inhaled sharply.

"Besides," Ginny continued, "she stole my trick. I'll get even yet."

Not before I do, June thought grimly. And she knew how to repay Ginny.

Each Southern Cross woman had a specific day to deposit her money in the bank. For June, Mondays were reserved for that function. Ginny always did her banking on Wednesdays. The Monday following her encounter with her employers, June deposited her money as usual. Afterward, she mailed a letter to one particular guest at a hotel near Cherry Creek. The guest's name was Jubal Bidwell.

Bidwell was a man feared in Denver's red-light district. Although there was no physical resemblance between him and Jimmy Morrow, the two men shared a common trait: they were both sadists. One of Bidwell's favorite pastimes was to buy a whore for the night and then beat her.

No respectable sporting house welcomed his business, including the Southern Cross. The previous month, Cross had kicked him out for beating one whore nearly to death.

Bidwell was the perfect weapon for June's revenge against Ginny.

Inside the envelope were twenty-five dollars and a note. The note asked Bidwell to snatch a certain whore and keep her off the streets for two days.

"You can do whatever you want with her, except kill her. She usually goes to the Rocky Mountain Bank on Fourteenth Street every Wednesday. Another twenty-five dollars will be mailed after you finish the job," June had written.

A cold smile formed on her lips. What Ginny had started, *she* was going to finish.

Wednesday morning dawned bright, and June was hopeful as she witnessed Ginny and Lucy depart for the bank. Two hours later, a distraught and bruised Lucy returned with disturbing news. Ginny had been snatched by a man wearing a sack over his head. Lucy had been shoved aside when she tried to help her friend.

Cross reported the incident to the city marshal.

"Too bad your girl didn't see who it was," the marshal said. He was a short, sturdy man, with narrow gray eyes and a large mustache. "It would have been a lot easier for me."

Cross's handsome face darkened with anger. "Sorry I can't help you on that score, Marshal. Meanwhile, why don't you try turning this town upside down and finding my girl!" It was plain the two men did not care for each other.

For two days, the lawman and his deputies scoured the city and the surrounding countryside for the abducted whore, with no luck. Then, on Saturday afternoon, Ginny was discovered in an abandoned shack just west of town. She was returned to the whorehouse, battered and bruised and with her dress in shreds.

"*Mon dieu!*" Therese whispered. "Who did that to

her?" Much to June's relief, Ginny was unable to tell. Her abductor had worn a hood during the entire time he had kept her, and he had said very little.

A week later, Denver received news of a shoot-out in Julesburg. One participant was former Denver resident Jubal Bidwell. He had ended up with two bullets in the head. June's secret remained safe.

After Ginny finally recovered, Cross and Therese suggested that the former beauty seek employment elsewhere. Her looks were no longer up to the standard quality of the house. Cross found her a berth at a seedy saloon down the street. A month later, a drunken teamster knifed her to death.

For the first time, June was consumed with guilt. Had her plan of revenge gone too far? Judging by Leanne's reaction, she began to suspect it had.

"Jesus, can you believe that?" Leanne whispered. She, June, and Clarice sat around the kitchen table, eating a late breakfast. Last night had been busy for the entire house. The trio had been the first downstairs and it was already eleven-thirty.

Clarice coolly dragged on the cigarette between her lips. A puff of gray smoke spiraled upward as she exhaled. "Why waste time feeling sorry for that woman? Hell, I couldn't care less what happened to her!"

"As much as I disliked Ginny, I wouldn't wish something like that on her."

"Leanne, she wouldn't have cared less if the same had happened to you. In fact, knowing Ginny, she would have laughed it off and thanked God it didn't

62

happened to her." Clarice took another drag on her cigarette. "Remember Fanny Wilson?"

"Yeah. Jimmy got to beat her up when she was caught moonlighting."

"Ginny was the one who tattled about Fanny's moonlighting in the first place. And I don't exactly recollect Cross or Therese saying we couldn't moonlight when I first joined."

Neither did June. In fact, she did not know of this rule until now.

"That poor girl just needed extra money for her folks back in Kansas, and that bitch Ginny snitched. Cross had Jimmy cripple the girl afterward. Now, do you still want to sit and moan over Ginny?"

The three women continued breakfast. Thelma had cooked a delicious meal of scrambled eggs, fried potatoes, ham, grits, and biscuits.

"Well, if you don't want to cry over Ginny," Leanne continued, "how about Tim McPherson?"

June glanced at her sharply. "What do you mean?"

"Someone killed his brother yesterday. One of the marshal's deputies told me."

Nathaniel McPherson had been robbed and murdered not far from the McPherson mines. The twenty thousand in gold he was carrying had disappeared. The county sheriff and his men were searching the entire countryside.

"Do they know who did it?" June asked.

"Bert Todd and his boys are the suspects. Some miner saw them not far from the McPherson mines yesterday afternoon. If I were Bert Todd, I wouldn't show my face in Denver for a long time."

"Knowing Bert Todd," Clarice retorted, "he'll probably show his face within a week. That is one crazy bastard."

Later that day, Tim showed up and requested June for the entire evening. A blank expression clouded his eyes, and his heart did not seem to be into any physical activity.

"I hope to God that son of a bitch is caught," Tim growled. A vengeful flame lit up his eyes. "That man took away the only family I ever had."

June asked if the sheriff was sure it was Bert Todd.

"One of our workers saw him and his men on the road that afternoon. I doubt if the law can catch them, considering the sheriff took so long to form a posse."

Poor Tim. June gently placed his head on her shoulder and began to stroke his hair. When Colonel St. John had mentioned Bert Todd, he had remarked that Harlin and another fellow had joined the outlaw. If that was true, it meant Harlin might be partly responsible for the death of Tim's brother.

Three weeks later, a short, wiry man entered the whorehouse parlor. His expensive wardrobe was obvious to the eye—a black sack coat that came to his thighs, a ruffled white shirt, black pants, and a brown silk waistcoat with a gold fob attached to it. The wide brim of his black hat partially hid his face.

He took off his hat. There was something familiar about that plain face and sherry-colored eyes. The stranger glanced around until his eyes fell upon June.

He slowly walked toward her. "Free for the evening, miss?"

June took note of the expensive outfit and pocket-watch and smiled. "My pleasure, sir. Follow me." And she guided him upstairs.

A half hour later the two heaved once more and separated. June got up and poured some water into a bowl. She asked her customer, a Mr. Ben Thomas of Independence, Missouri, if he would like something to eat.

"Sure thing, darling. All this work can get a man hungry," he drawled.

June smiled again, put on her robe, and left the room. First, she went to her living room next door and wrote a short note. Downstairs, she asked Thelma to prepare supper for her customer. She found the very person she was looking for just outside the kitchen. "Eddie, I need to speak to you for a minute," she told the houseboy, dragging him outside the back door and into the cold evening. Eddie was a skinny, dark twelve-year-old, with appealing wide brown eyes. "How would you like to make twenty dollars?"

Those brown eyes widened even further. "How much?"

"Twenty. All you have to do is take this note to the sheriff's office for me."

"The sheriff ain't coming here, is he? Mr. Allen don't like the law inside unless they's a customer or he asks for them."

"Don't worry, the sheriff won't be coming inside. Just give this note to him. Please?" June gave the boy her most appealing look and he caved in.

She watched with satisfaction as the boy's thin legs scampered around the building.

The moment the man had taken his hat off in the parlor, June had known who he was: Bert Todd. She had seen his likeness posted outside the marshal's office one day on her way to the bank.

In about thirty minutes or so, Bert Todd was going to be arrested.

"Did you enjoy yourself, honey?" June asked. Todd was finishing the last of the roast venison Thelma had cooked for him.

The outlaw sighed. "Sure did. I haven't had a meal like that in quite a while."

"Oh?"

Todd hesitated for a second. "I haven't been in town for a while. Just struck gold recently." He placed the tray on one of the side tables and flicked open his pocketwatch. "Well, sweetheart, looks like my time is up. It's been fun though."

In a swift motion, he got out of bed and gave June a hard kiss. "Don't worry your pretty little head though. I'll be back."

I wouldn't count on it, June thought smugly. She received her twenty-five dollars from the outlaw and within a few minutes he was dressed and gone.

It was not long before a commotion was heard from outside on the street. June heard Todd's voice cry out, "What the hell's going on?"

"Bert Todd!" The voice belonged to the county

sheriff. "You're under arrest for robbery and murder...."

A loud scuffle interrupted the sheriff. And then there were gunshots. One of the women from inside the whorehouse screamed. June, along with several other occupants, rushed outside and joined the crowd on the sidewalk, several yards away from the action. The marshal and his men, who were there to help the sheriff, ordered the crowd to disperse. Before departing, June managed to get a glimpse of Bert Todd's dead body lying on the street in a pool of blood.

A tall, lanky man with fair hair glanced at June with interest. She was the only spectator left. "Well, there he is," said the sheriff. "Thanks for the tip." He eyed the corpse dispassionately. "At least I'll be spared wasting more money searching for this bastard."

"Speaking of money, Sheriff...," June began.

"You can pick up the reward in my office tomorrow."

News of Bert Todd's demise traveled fast throughout Denver, and it appeared on the front page of the *Rocky Mountain View* newspaper. Some of the Southern Cross ladies were at the breakfast table reading the paper's morning edition.

The article gave a full report of Todd's death, his past crimes, what he was accused of, and his known accomplices who were still at large. It did leave out certain details—such as the fact that Todd had spent the evening at the whorehouse. And it did not mention June's name.

"June." Thelma entered the kitchen. She looked scared. "Mr. Allen and Miz Therese want to see you."

The other whores stared at June. Everyone knew Todd had been June's customer last night. She stared back. Had they guessed that she was responsible for the outlaw's death? Even worse, had Cross or Therese?

An hour later, a washed and fully dressed June entered the office downstairs. Both Cross and Therese were seated at their desks. And Jimmy was standing to the right of Cross's mahogany desk, flexing his fist and wearing that strange smile of his. She caught sight of the figure standing near Therese and nearly gasped. It was young Eddie.

The boy stole a look at June before quickly leaving the room.

Cross drawled, "I reckon you can guess why we ordered you in here, June."

She remained silent.

"Let me put it to you this way. Therese and I don't tolerate liars, thieves, or snitches in this house. Do I make myself clear?" His dark eyes bored into hers.

Therese cleared her throat. June turned to the madam. Her eyes glittered green and hard. Like emeralds. "Last night Jimmy went to Grogan's for cigars. Imagine his surprise when he spotted Eddie coming out of the sheriff's office."

"The next thing he knew," Cross continued with a slightly raised voice, "Bert Todd was getting his balls shot off a couple of feet away from the Southern

Cross. Now, as you saw, we had a little talk with Eddie."

"And?" June said. It was remarkable that she managed to remain so calm.

The others were just as surprised as she was by her response.

"And he told us you sent him to the sheriff with a note. You snitched on Todd, didn't you?"

June realized it was useless to lie. She took a deep breath. "Yes, I did."

Therese got up and thrust her angry face in front of June's. "That's it? That is all you have to say?" She slapped June's face.

"Now Therese, honey. Let's not lose our temper." Cross took a cigar from a box on his desk. "June, we have a thriving business here. We don't snitch on customers. It brings on retaliation in the worst possible way. And we could lose customers seeking privacy."

June found his condescending manner tiresome. She remarked, "Mister Cross, most of your customers are quality folks. Bert Todd was a thief and a murderer. And he's now dead. Since most fellas like him go elsewhere for a poke, why should you be concerned for him?"

She immediately regretted her words. In an unusual display of temper, Cross picked up the tin box of cigars and threw it across the room, barely missing her.

"Don't you get it, you stupid whore? I don't give a damn what Todd was! All I know is he was a customer, and a customer always come first! If Therese or I cared about their morals, we wouldn't have any business!"

June flinched before his anger. She saw the easy grin on Jimmy's face widen. Deep breaths helped her calm her nerves. "I expect you want me to leave." She tossed a bag of coins on Cross's table. "Here's the five hundred you paid Harlin, plus interest."

"Oh no, June," said Therese with a shake of her head. "You will have to pay a little extra for the trouble you caused us." She nodded at the bouncer. "Jimmy."

Jimmy stepped forward, slipping a pair of brass knuckles over his right hand. Then he stopped. In June's hand was a small Smith and Allen pepperbox. It was a present she had received from Tim after he had heard about her last visit to the office.

"Hold on, Jimmy. You've hit me for the last time, you hear?" There was no mistaking the menace in June's voice. Jimmy seemed to have recognized it. His fear was apparent in his eyes.

"Put the gun down, June," Cross ordered.

"Shut up! I ain't leaving this office with a busted face. You want a little extra for that son of a bitch Todd? Here!" With her left hand, she deftly pulled out a small pouch from her skirt pocket. "Fifty dollars should be enough, I reckon. Now, I got some money to collect. Anyone who follows me dies."

The pepperbox still in her hand, June slowly backed toward the door. "Bye, everyone. Can't rightly say it's been nice knowing you." She opened the door with her free hand and slipped out.

June was grateful she had the foresight to pack her belongings before meeting with Cross and Therese. Her two carpetbags were still next to the front door. She picked them up, glanced around the front hall for the last time, and left the whorehouse. It was time to move on, anyhow, she thought. There was more important business waiting for her.

Chapter 5

Smokey Hill Trail, Kansas, January 1866.

Two days out of Denver, the Overland Trail Express stagecoach rolled along the flat, cold ground of western Kansas. Despite the sporadic trouble many travelers still experienced from Indians, the coach was spared from attack on this trip.

The former slave, former army laundress, and now former prostitute was on her way to Ellsworth City to find a man named Artemus Lake. According to Tim McPherson, he was the person who could help her find Harlin.

Not long after she had left the Southern Cross, June went to the sheriff's office to pick up her reward for turning in Bert Todd. She had just tucked the roll of greenbacks totaling a thousand dollars into her reticule, when she spotted a familiar face on the bulletin board. *Harlin*. It and three others hung next to a picture of Bert Todd.

"Are these the fellows who rode with Todd?" she asked the sheriff. June's finger pointed at Harlin's likeness.

The sheriff walked over to the bulletin board. "Yep. That's Harlin Mason you're pointing at. The others are Ben Carlson, Phil O'Keefe, and Adam Jenkins. Last I heard, they were all in Kansas. Wanted for cattle rustling, I believe." He laughed. "Funny. If Todd had stuck with them, he would still be alive."

"Kansas, huh?"

"You're going after them?" The lanky, blond man stared at June with disbelief.

"Of course not," June said quietly, returning the lawman's stare with a cool smile.

Then June bid the sheriff good-bye and left for the stagecoach station. There she learned that a stage for Kansas was departing around four o'clock. Plenty of time for her to get her business in order before leaving.

She went to the bank and closed her account, then went to another bank and opened one there, depositing her earnings and the reward, an amount that added up to two thousand dollars. She kept a hundred dollars for travel in a money belt. It was two-thirty in the afternoon when she finally went to Tim's house.

Since it was the middle of the day, there was a good chance that the miner would not be at home. June had intended to leave a note and go, but when she knocked on the door of Tim's house, a two-story affair with a veranda, he appeared in the doorway.

"June!" He seemed surprised to see her. "What are you doing here?" Once inside, June told him about her part in Bert Todd's capture and her departure from the Southern Cross.

"So you are finally leaving that place, huh? What are you going to do now?"

"Go after Harlin." June said it matter-of-factly.

"After all these years?"

"A year and a half."

"But you don't even know where to find him!"

"He's in Kansas. I learned that from the sheriff."

"Jesus, woman! You just can't go roaming about the country looking for one man. You haven't been outside Denver since before the end of the war! And you don't know a thing about surviving on the plains."

"I'll learn. Or find someone who can teach me." June realized she was being stubborn, but she could not help it. "Look Tim," she said before the miner could open his mouth, "I know all the arguments you're going to make. But when Harlin left me at the Southern Cross like that..., *sold* me for five hundred dollars, I swore I'd get even."

Tim only muttered, "Jesus Christ." Then he sighed. "I knew that bastard had hurt you. Hell, he and his friends hurt me too, but I didn't realize it went that deep with you."

June sighed. "After my family was sold, I had no one but Martha—the housekeeper—and Harlin. No one else. The other slaves never liked me, I reckon."

Suddenly, the lonely days at Devonfield, right after

her family was sold, came back to her. She had been just too different for the other slaves to tolerate. Being a slave had been bad enough. Being disliked by her fellow slaves, even when she was only twelve years old, had been intolerable.

June continued, "Now Martha's dead. Harlin double-crossed me. And I have no one left."

"There's me," Tim said.

June smiled. "There's you."

"And Clarice and Leanne."

"I can't see them anymore. I can't stay here in Denver. And I can't come back here, at least not until there's been time for Mr. Cross to forget about the gun I pulled on him."

Tim winced. "I see your point." He sighed. "Okay. If you're going after this Harlin, you'll need a good man to help you." He got a piece of paper and wrote on it.

"Here," he said, handing the paper to June. "This is a fella I know in Ellsworth. A bounty hunter named Artemus Lake. He used to be a cavalry scout during the war."

"Would he mind helping a colored woman?"

"Hell no! Arty has a different way of judging people. Besides, he once rode with John Brown."

"That's a relief." June slipped the piece of paper into her purse. She looked up and noticed the sad look on the miner's face. "Oh come on, Tim! It might be awhile, but I'll be back."

"Yeah, yeah. Can I at least have one last kiss for old times sake?"

The two friends leaned forward and kissed each other. It was a brief but emotion-filled kiss. "Take care of yourself, Tim."

"You too, Junebug."

June grimaced at the name, smiled briefly, and waved good-bye.

Two days later, she sat uncomfortably inside the stagecoach, freezing from the cold wind blowing outside. June glared at the window that had been opened by a fellow passenger, a red-faced stout man who had earlier complained about the lack of air. *Jesus! Why couldn't the man just sit outside behind the driver? He would get all the air he wanted.*

Perhaps she should not complain too much. Unlike the driver who had taken her and Harlin to Denver, this one did not force her to sit outside on top of the stage. The Overland Express Stage Company did not have a racial policy. Seating arrangements were left to the discrimination of the individual drivers.

As the vehicle rolled east, June observed the thin layer of snow blanketing the flat land. The coach followed the Smokey Hill River straight into June's destination, a town situated on the river's north bank called Ellsworth.

"Whoa!" the driver said, forcing the coach to stop. "Ellsworth, folks! This is a meal stop. The coach'll be continuing east in one hour!"

It was now dusk and June figured she would need to obtain a room somewhere before locating Artemus Lake. But where? After collecting her gear, she strolled along the muddy street, hoping to find someone who could suggest a hotel or boardinghouse where she could stay.

Like many other towns that had sprung up along the frontier, Ellsworth was a motley collection of one-story shacks, buildings with false fronts, and large tents. Shabby-looking buffalo hunters in their robes, teamsters holding coiled whips, sharply-dressed gamblers and tricksters, and uniformed army men trudged along the streets, searching for the right saloon or whorehouse to spend their lonely nights. June tightened the coat around her, attempting to ward off the winter air. One glance at the dreary scene before her gave June the feeling that perhaps the West was better off unsettled.

"June?" A familiar voice cried out. "June Daley?" She turned around. A tall, handsome black man wearing a shaggy coat and the hat of a cavalry trooper walked toward her. "June! Don't you remember me? From Atchison?"

The face came back to her. "Of course! Charlie Taylor! What are you doing here?"

"I'm on furlough. Again." Both the soldier and the woman smiled. The last time the two had met, Charlie had just ended his furlough and was on his way back to report for duty. "I was visiting an old friend of my father's."

"You stayed in the army?"

Charlie shrugged sheepishly. "You know me. Can't resist a uniform. Where you staying?"

"I just got in town."

"I reckon the stage you just got off is the one I

have to catch in fifty minutes." He took her arm. "Come on, I'll take you to where I've been staying. There might be a room for you."

Still the gentleman, June thought with a smile as she allowed the trooper to guide her through the streets.

Miss Wendell's boardinghouse was a two-story house located near the edge of town. The middle-aged spinster, a skinny woman with faded blonde hair and cheerful expression, gave June the room Charlie had just vacated. "Supper will be ready in five minutes. Hannah is a fine cook."

The two friends went into the dining room. "I thought you had a stage to catch," June said.

"I still got forty minutes. Might as well get a bite before it leaves."

While they waited for the buffalo steaks Charlie had ordered, the soldier recalled the months since they had met. After the war ended, he had been discharged from the First Kansas Volunteers. He went back to his family's farm in Nebraska, but the war's excitement had made him restless.

Just four months ago, Charlie had received word that the army was forming new colored regiments to serve out west. He had enlisted in the Tenth Calvary, a colored regiment under Colonel Benjamin Grierson, now stationed at Fort Leavenworth.

"When the Colonel found out I was a veteran, he decided to give me more stripes. I might be a sergeant the next time we meet," Charlie announced proudly.

June smiled. She was happy for Charlie. Yet she could not imagine anyone thrilled over being in the army—especially Charlie, since he already had a home.

He asked, "So, what are you doing here at Ellsworth?"

"I'm looking for someone. A man name Artemus Lake."

Charlie's eyebrows knitted together in thought. "Name sounds familiar. Why are you looking for him?"

June paused for a minute. "To help me find Harlin. I haven't seen him since a week after you and I last saw each other." She then told the soldier about Harlin's betrayal and her months at the Southern Cross. She left nothing out.

Looking as if a snake had bit him, Charlie stared at June with his mouth wide open. "My God!" he exclaimed. "Jesus Christ! I was right about him after all!"

"Yeah, I know."

"Wait a minute, you said he used to ride with Bert Todd? Damn, June! That boy was one of the worst kind on these plains! And if Harlin once rode with him...."

"Harlin might be another Bert Todd. I also found that out a long time ago. That's why I'm looking for this Mr. Lake. A friend in Denver told me he could help me."

"You don't know what this Artemus Lake is like, June. It's best you get on with your life and forget all this revenge stuff."

June stared at Charlie. "And do what?"

"Well..., you can work for the army again."

"Washing and cleaning for them? Forget it! I had enough of them bluebellies back in Tennessee!"

Charlie glanced past her shoulder. "I'll be there."

He had said it so simply, June almost missed the implication, until she looked into his eyes.

She tried to be as gentle as possible. "Look, Charlie, I like you very much, but I won't work for the army again. Not even for you. Besides, I don't know you that well."

They left it at that until their supper was over. Later, June and Charlie went back out on the street and headed for the station. They barely said a word.

When they reached the Overland station, June turned around and brushed his chin with her finger. "Charlie? I don't want us to split up with you mad at me. I want us to stay friends. But you have to understand, I've got this fire raging inside me right now. I'm not good company. And the only way to put it out is for me to find Harlin and get even."

"June," Charlie squeaked out before she placed a finger on his lips.

She smiled brightly. Without bothering to pay attention to the others surrounding them, she placed a gentle kiss at the side of his mouth. "I'll be seeing you around, Charlie Taylor." June kissed him again and left.

After the stage journey and her encounter with Charlie Taylor, June was exhausted. It was no surprise that June slept later than she had intended the next morning. She glanced at the fob watch on the table beside her. *Damn! It was half past ten.* She should have been awake over two hours earlier.

After a quick breakfast, she headed for the town marshal's office. When she got there, she asked how she could find Artemus Lake.

"He's got a small spread a couple of miles east of here," the lawman informed her. He stared at her curiously. "You got some business with him?"

June wanted to tell him to mind his own business, but it was the law she was speaking to. "A friend of his in Denver wanted me to look him up. Thanks for the information." She started to leave.

"Last I heard he was away from home," the marshal added. "Don't know if he's back or not. Try checking at Tucker's store. The old man there might know."

"Thanks, Marshal. I'll do that!"

Tucker's general store was a one-story wooden building with a porch in front. A group of undesirable-looking fellows hung around smoking and indulging in the usual conversation that was popular with their type.

Before June could place a foot on the first step, she saw a figure ahead of her, a black man, already on the wide porch. He looked familiar.

One of the white loiterers stopped in front of the man. "Hey! Your kind ain't welcome here. Why don't you try that kraut's place up the street? He don't mind serving niggers." Laughter followed.

June saw the black man's figure stiffen. He whirled around and stalked away. She saw a glimpse of the grizzled man's face, tight with anger. For some reason, memories of a steamboat flashed through her mind.

She started to turn away when a hand gripped her forearm. "You going somewhere, gal?" June's heart started to beat rapidly.

"Like you said, mister, colored ain't allowed here."

The man who gripped her arm reeked of animal skin. Judging from the filthy buckskins and hat he wore, June guessed he was a buffalo hunter. A heavy brown beard dominated his face. Brown eyes and yellow teeth peeped out from his grimy face.

"In your case, I'll make an exception," he said with an easy smile. "In fact, you can service me." His fellow companions broke into raucous laughter.

"Please, sir, let me go. I'm not interested."

The hunter refused to listen. His eyes narrowed dangerously. "Now, I'll be damned if I'm gonna be refused by some nigger wench."

The pepperbox that had proved so reliable in Denver was suddenly in June's hand, aimed at her harasser. "Let go of me, you greasy bastard, or I'll put a hole in your stomach," she hissed coldly. "Now!"

The combination of the gun, June's tone, and her flat, angry eyes convinced the buffalo hunter to do as she said. She stepped away from the steps and slowly walked away.

Someone remarked, "Hey, Henry! Reckon you should've taken a bath. Considering you smell like a buffalo wallow, it's no wonder the little darling turned you down." The men on the porch now concentrated their laughter at the hunter.

As June turned back to see if she was being followed, she noticed that Henry had turned red as a pickled beet. Yet his eyes remained on her. *Oh God, a new enemy.* She would have to keep her eyes open while in Ellsworth.

June eventually learned from a livery stable owner that Artemus Lake was due back at his ranch that day. Lake's place was a two-hour walk from town, so June bought a horse from the stable, a mare with reddish-brown coloring named Rusty. Her father had been a groom at Devonfield and taught June how to ride when she was a child. June had no problem in developing a rapport with the spirited mare.

After a change into shirt and pants, it took June at least an hour to reach Lake's ranch north of the Smokey Hill River. It was a small spread with a dilapidated one-story cabin, a stable right behind. The corral was situated several yards west of the stable. Cottonwood trees, possibly planted by Lake himself, formed a path to the ranch's front yard.

June dismounted from Rusty and walked to the cabin's front door. She knocked. "Hello?" she called out. There was no answer.

She tried opening the door but it was locked. The corral was empty so June headed for the stables. *Empty. A ranch with no horses?* It did not make sense. As June started toward the empty stalls, a grimy hand clamped her mouth, stifling a scream. Steel arms wrapped around her body.

"Well, well! If it ain't the little nigger gal who turned me down." It was Henry, the buffalo hunter. "I reckon I'll find out just how good you are for me. Next time you point a gun at someone, honey, you best pull the trigger. Now, come on!"

June struggled desperately to escape from Henry's iron grip. All she succeeded in doing was having herself forced on down on the ground. Pieces of hay clung to her clothing as Henry pinned her to the ground and straddled her.

She tried biting the buffalo hunter's hand. Henry yelled out in pain. "You stupid bitch!" he said viciously, slapping her across the face. She felt warm blood trickling down her chin.

The hunter then ripped open her shirt, sending buttons flying into the hay. Next her bodice came apart and gnarled hands began fondling her breasts roughly.

June let out a piercing scream.

"Ain't gonna do you any good, honey!" Henry crowed. "There ain't nobody around to help ya."

By some bizarre fate, a loud noise punctuated his last words. Blood spattered on June's face as the hunter arched and dropped on top of her.

With a gasp, June pushed the dead body off her and sat up. Approaching her was the grizzled black man from Ellsworth, carrying a smoking pistol.

"Don't I know you, girl?" were the man's first words. Unable to speak, June continued to sit on the ground, panting heavily. "What's your name?"

Finally she spoke. "June. June Daley." She took a deep breath and exclaimed, "Damn! That was mighty close, wasn't it?"

"Would you have preferred me to wait until he had his carrot stuck in you?"

"I reckon not." June glanced at her ripped blouse and realized she was exposed to this man. She covered herself with her arms and stared at him warily. "Thanks for your help, mister."

"Levi Walker. I saw that bastard following you out of town."

Levi Walker? The name seemed vaguely familiar.

Levi peered at June closely. "Hey, don't I know you from somewhere?"

"Well, have you ever been to Denver?" June replied.

"Denver? I'll be damned! That's it! You and some buck had left the *Bonnie Union* back in Atchison! During the spring of sixty-four, as I recollect!"

Now June remembered. The mountain man to whom Harlin had been nasty. He had warned them of the trouble in Denver. "Yeah, that was me. I remember you too."

Curious brown eyes appraised her. "What you doing here back in Kansas? As I recall, you and that friend of yours was heading for Denver."

"We got there. We separated afterward." June stood up, her arms still over her chest. "You happen to know a Mr. Artemus Lake?"

"Yeah, this is his place. You looking for him?"

"I wanted him to find somebody for me."

86

"Oh. Well, let's see if he's here."

June gave Levi a quizzled stare.

"Come on, girl."

The former mountain man led June farther into the stable. "I saw your horse outside, just before you screamed." He suddenly stopped. Sprawled against a stack of hay was a man with an enormous black mustache and curly dark hair. In the center of his forehead was a red hole formed by a bullet.

Chapter 6

Ellsworth, Kansas, 1866.

June sat in the marshal's office, feeling desolate as
Levi explained their discovery of Lake's body.
Whoever had stolen the bounty hunter's horses had
ruined her only chance of any decent help in searching for Harlin.

The marshal turned to June and asked why she was
so hot on finding Lake. At first taken by surprise by
the lawman's suspicious tone, June recovered and
spun a tale about hiring Lake's services to find a
brother she had not seen since the war. She did not
want to encourage the marshal's suspicions even further by mentioning Harlin. She added that a friend in
Denver mentioned Lake as the man to help her.

Levi mentioned that Lake's entire herd was missing from the ranch.

The possibility of rustlers could not be ruled out. June's head snapped up at the mention of rustlers. Weren't Harlin and his friends wanted for that very crime here in Kansas?

"Who do you think? The Mason and Carlson bunch?" the marshal asked.

Levi answered, "Could be. But they ain't the only ones operating rustling outfits. Lot of those old guerrilla riders are terrorizing the state these days."

The marshal nodded. June was amazed by how highly the lawman seemed to regard Levi's opinion.

"As for Henry Bell, I shot him. He was attacking the girl," Levi continued, nodding at June.

The marshal accepted Levi's story and allowed him and June to leave. The pair stepped outside into the street.

"How come he believed you?" June asked.

"Simple. As much as they don't like having me around, folks here know me. I've been around these parts longer than this town's been here, and they know that. Besides, some white folks ain't all that bad. Sometimes."

June had another question. "I heard you mention rustlers to the marshal. Do you know who they might be?"

"Hell, girl! There's so many of 'em operating in Kansas these days, it would be impossible to find out. Let alone catch 'em. Besides, they usually hightail for the territory if the heat gets too close."

"Yeah." June turned to Levi with a grateful smile. "Well, thanks for your help. That man would have slit my throat after doing God knows what to me." She started to walk away.

"Hold on!" Levi grabbed her arm and stopped her. "Where you going?"

"To get my things and head south."

"What for?"

"Like I told you, to look for someone."

"Your missing brother, perhaps?" Levi said with a cocked brow. "The only person I recollect you being with is that fellow from the *Bonnie Union*. And you two didn't look like brother and sister to me." Hard brown eyes bored deep into June's. "Now who might be heading south into Indian Territory that you want so badly?"

June remained silent and looked away. Her eyes fell upon a freight driver trying to coax a team of oxen through the muddy streets. Despite her silence, the former mountain man guessed.

"Jesus Christ!" he exclaimed, eyes wide open in disbelief. "It's Harlin Mason you're looking for! No wonder you were so interested about the location of horse thieves! He's that boy from the steamboat!"

"That's right," June answered.

"Wh…why do you want to find him? He's the last person you want to be near!"

"It's a long story."

It did not take June as long as she thought to tell him. Back inside her room at the boardinghouse, she packed her belongings while she related the past year and a half of her life.

"I can understand why you want to go after that

bastard," Levi replied, "but I tell you right now, you are in no shape to do it."

"That's why I came here to find Artemus Lake. Only he's dead, so there's no one left but me." June was annoyed that Levi had offered criticism instead of the sympathy she had expected.

Levi barked a short, harsh laugh. "Yeah, I can see you in the territory all right. Shit, girl! They'll eat you alive down there! No wonder that son-of-a-bitch Bell found you so easily! You don't know nothing about surviving out here."

"What do you suggest I do?"

"Come with me. I work for a couple who run a stage station on the trail."

"I beg your pardon?" June wanted to tell the man what he could do with his offer. "May I ask how working at some stagecoach station's gonna help me find Harlin?"

Before June could stop him, Levi grabbed hold of her carpetbag. "'Cause while you're working there, I'm gonna teach you how to survive in this land." He started for the door. "Now, let's go."

The flat plains seemed to stretch forever as June and Levi rode southeast. Not a sign of life stirred across the barren horizon. Kansas in January. Still, June felt more alive than she ever had in Denver or at Devonfield. The west throve like a health tonic inside her.

Since leaving Ellsworth, neither she nor Levi had talked very much. Yet the mountain man's presence in Kansas prompted a question in June's mind. She broke the silence and asked, "What are you doing working at a way station? I thought you owned a ranch."

"I still do," Levi answered. "My oldest boy runs it now. My wife died just a year ago. She was a Cheyenne woman. She came down with a fever and was starting to recover, but then news of Sand Creek came in and...." He heaved a sigh. "Well, she just gave up living."

"Why did she...?" The odd expression in Levi's eyes cut June short. "Oh. I see. Some of her kin got killed, huh?"

"Most of 'em, including her mama and sisters. I just couldn't stand being at the ranch with her gone, so I left. Put Carson and his wife in charge. I've only been back once."

He sounded so sad that June's heart nearly broke just listening to him.

"Course, Mister and Miz Lynch ain't bad," Levi continued. "They run the station. Nice folks but too trusting. I can't see them lasting very long out here."

The orange sun glared from behind the riders as they arrived at the small way station just south of a small ridge. The Lynch station consisted of a wide one-story cabin with a sod roof, a smaller cabin situated right behind, a stable also with a sod roof, and a corral filled with grazing horses.

Nelson and Hannah Lynch were originally from western Ohio. According to Levi, the couple had migrated out here eleven years ago with their two sons. After surviving the pre-war violence and three years of civil war that torched Kansas, the farm finally went under from an attack by rebel guerrilla riders. The stock had been driven off and the barn burned. There had been no one to help them because the couple's sons were both serving in the Union army. The Lynches had to hide in the cellar to prevent certain death at the hands of the guerrillas.

Their youngest son had died during the battle for Atlanta, a year and a half ago. The surviving son had married, moved to Grand Island in Nebraska Territory, and opened a dry goods store. Unwilling to put Kansas behind them, the Lynches tried to save their farm. Unfortunately, luck eluded them.

Friends later informed them of the Overland–Pike's Peak Stagecoach Express search for someone to run its way station fifty miles east of Ellsworth. The Lynches had been there for nine months when Levi first rode in.

A tall, stocky man with salt-and-pepper hair forming a fringe around his dome-shaped head approached the incoming riders. "Ah, Levi. Who is this young lady with you?" He peered at June with curious blue eyes.

June liked Lynch at first sight. He seemed friendly enough. So did his wife. Hannah Lynch was a petite woman whose brunette hair was streaked with gray. Her delicate face revealed signs of ravage from past hardships and prairie living.

"This is June Daley, Mister Lynch. I found her in Ellsworth looking for a job," the ex-mountain man

94

easily lied. June was grateful he had decided not to reveal her past.

His next lie, however, drew a sharp glance from her. "She had nowhere else to go and I found her about to offer herself at, you know, one of those places of the evening,"—June was sure he meant a whorehouse—"so I brought her with me."

Mrs. Lynch approached June with a sympathetic air. "You poor child," she cooed. "It's a good thing Levi found you. You can help me clean around the station."

Still annoyed by Levi's lie, June smiled weakly. "Yes, ma'am."

"Do you cook?" Mr. Lynch asked. He glanced lovingly at his wife. "Mrs. Lynch is a wonderful wife, June, but not much of a cook."

"Oh, Nelson!" Mrs. Lynch laughed, obviously not put off by the insult.

"Yes, sir. I'm a pretty good cook," June answered.

"Good! Then you're hired. Your pay is a dollar a week. You can sleep in the small room inside the station house."

June shot another glance in Levi's direction. A dollar a week? She had made more than that as an army laundress and cook during the war.

The mountain man disregarded June's dismay. "Thank you, sir, ma'am. You don't know how much this means to her."

The hell I do! June thought darkly. She wished she had never listened to him.

Despite her initial frustration at being talked into staying, June eased quickly into the station's routine within days. Whenever a stagecoach stopped by, it was she who quickly prepared the food while Mrs. Lynch served it to the passengers. Other than that, she cooked the daily meals, helped Mrs. Lynch clean the station house and mend clothes, and helped Levi and Mr. Lynch with the care of the horses. Her free time was devoted to learning a series of lessons from the former mountain man.

The Colt revolver felt heavy in June's hands as she aimed it at a row of empty bottles situated on a small table in front of the cottonwood tree.

"OK, June, fire!" Levi ordered.

With her eyes closed, she pulled the trigger. The gun gave a tremendous kick. Repeatedly she fired until all the bullets were gone. June opened her eyes.

Levi took the gun from her hands. "Not bad. You actually managed to hit one…, and with your eyes closed."

A wave of embarrassment swept over June.

Her tutor added, "Next time, try to keep your eyes open. Maybe you'll see what you're shooting." He loaded the revolver and handed it to her. "Now, try again."

"You sure you want me to attack you with this?" June asked one cold afternoon in late February. She held a sharp bowie knife in her right hand.

Levi stood opposite her with both hands on his hips.

"Yeah." He crouched into position. "Now, come on; go for me!"

The two circled each other warily. June slashed the knife about as expertly as she could. Just as she was ready to set upon him, Mrs. Lynch's voice rang out, "Stage coming!"

June glanced up and, before she knew it, Levi had gripped her wrist, forced the knife out of her hand, and kicked her legs out from under her. She fell flat onto the ground.

"Never," he said, looking down at her, "let yourself get taken off guard like that again. Especially when you're in danger. If I had been someone else, you would have been dead."

June and Levi sat upon the ground in front of a roaring campfire. It was mid-May and the air was filled with the fresh, sweet smell of spring. By now, their relationship had drifted into a parent–child friendship.

Levi spoke a few words in a strange tongue.

"What on earth did you just say?" June asked.

"I said I'm gonna to teach you the Cheyenne tongue."

"What do I need to speak Injun for? Kansas is a state now."

"June, there are other folks on these plains who don't speak good English. You know, Cheyenne, Arapaho, Sioux, Kiowa, Kansa. Ever heard of them?"

"I can't learn some new language!" June protested.

Levi sighed. "There are two basic tongues you gotta

learn—Algonquian and Siouxan. Many plains tribes speak 'em and not all of 'em know English. Just because Kansas is a state don't mean all of them are now gone. Now, let's start on Cheyenne, which is part of the Algonquian tongue."

June sat on Rusty with ease while Levi examined her with a critical eye. "Not bad," he said. "You're a pretty good rider. Who taught you?"

"My daddy. He was Massa George's groom at Devonfield. He taught me how to ride before I was ten."

"You do your daddy proud." Levi mounted his horse. "Considering the way you sit on a horse, he must have been a pretty good rider himself."

"Massa George used to breed racing horses. It was Daddy who trained them. Besides," she added with a laugh, "he was just as good as you."

Levi scowled briefly and began the riding lessons.

June at first protested. "I don't need riding lessons!"

"What I'm gonna teach you are ways your daddy never knew; now, shut up!" He taught June how to ride at full gallop while shooting with a pistol or revolver and how to ride bareback. He also taught her a certain little trick used by his late wife's people. "Watch me," he instructed.

Levi cantered several yards toward the east. He then turned around and rode toward June at full gallop. As he passed by her, he half-slid off the saddle—left foot in the stirrup and right leg over the horn.

Levi's torso was level with the horse's left flank.

June stared with disbelief. He didn't really expect her to learn that! Did he?

The July sun blazed down on the little stagecoach station with great intensity as June brought Rusty out of the stable. She and Levi were leaving to purchase supplies. Since the mail and fresh horses were also on their shopping list, the two headed not for Ellsworth but for Atchison, the stage line's headquarters.

The late spring and early summer had brought wagon trains through their area, traveling west along the Smokey Hill Trail. Since it was July, the numbers had dwindled to only a few dozen wagons. But still, June and Levi wanted to avoid the traffic, so they took a parallel route just north of the train.

"Late starters," Levi remarked with a shake of his head. "Should have been out of here two months ago. Grazing grass is going to be low from earlier travelers. And if they're heading beyond the Rockies, good luck."

June asked why.

"Are you kidding? By the time they reach the Rockies, they'll be snowed in. They might have to winter at some fort."

They arrived at Atchison within three days. Since it was twilight when they reached the small city, they decided to stay overnight at the same boardinghouse where June and Harlin had stayed some two years before.

After supper, the two sat in the parlor while June

wrote a letter to Charlie Taylor. During the past five months she had written him two letters. Levi watched as she placed the sheets of paper into the envelope. "I didn't know you could write," he commented. "Who's it going to?"

"A friend of mine. He's in the army," June answered.

"Oh? Maybe I know him. What's his name?"

"Charlie. Charlie Taylor."

"I know that boy! I last saw him in Ellsworth the day before we ran into each other. I got to know him about twelve years ago when I guided his family into Nebraska. Nice boy." Levi peered at June closer. "You two courting?"

June shook her head. As much as she liked Charlie, she found him a little too priggish for her tastes. And she harbored no ambition to be an army wife.

The former mountain man surprised her by answering, "Good. He's not your type anyway. Charlie's a decent boy, but you two would be at each other's throats within a month. You're just a little too strong-willed and carefree for him, and he's not very tolerant of unconventional people. Now, if I were to pick a man for you, I would suggest my boy."

June smirked. "I thought your boy was married."

"My oldest is. I got another one, Joshua. He's a lot more quiet than Carson, but I reckon he could handle you." Levi smiled.

June's smirk grew wider. "I doubt it very much."

"Josh is a quiet boy. A 'gentleman,' one would say. But a lot tougher than one thinks. Too many people have thought otherwise and have been unpleasantly surprised. Including Charlie Taylor. It's probably why they don't like each other, I reckon."

"Is Joshua at the ranch with your other boy?"

"No. Believe it or not he took up bounty hunting after the war. Don't care much for his new profession but," Levi sighed, "he likes it and he's got a good partner, despite the man being an ex-Reb."

A bounty hunter, huh? Joshua Walker seemed like the right man for June to look up. Perhaps Levi's son could help her find Harlin. She kept the thought to herself and stored it in a corner of her mind for future use.

When June and Levi returned to the way station, they brought with them supplies, new horses, and news. Just before leaving Atchison, they had discovered that the army commander at Fort Leavenworth, William Sherman of the famed march through Georgia, was in the midst of treaty negotiations with several of the plains tribes.

"Considering what he did to Georgia and the Carolinas, God help the tribes if they don't take up that fella's offer," Levi remarked after he had informed the Lynches.

"Really, Mr. Walker!" Mrs. Lynch rebuked. "You hardly know the man."

Her husband added, "Bill Sherman is a fine fellow. And a top soldier." The Lynches' oldest son had served with the general during the war.

The couple's rebukes failed to deflect Levi. "Yeah,

and a ruthless bastard for sure. There's probably gonna be blood on the plains anyway. Just like Colorado."

The mountain man had predicted accurately. Bloodshed between the Plains Indians and the U.S. Army did explode, despite the treaty negotiations. Stories of white settlements and tribal villages under attack reached the station. Although the violence that flared up never affected the station, eastbound stagecoaches arrived with passengers shaken from attacks. There were several times during the late summer and early fall when Mrs. Lynch and June had to care for the wounded.

Spring 1867 arrived with the news that Bill Sherman had ordered the commander of the Missouri River Division, another Civil War general named Winfield Hancock, to inflict full-scale war upon the Plains Indians. According to Levi, this General Hancock had a fierce reputation. "There's an ex-slave at Rock Creek who told me that, although a gentleman, this man was a fighter."

For once, a stagecoach from the east delivered some alarming news for the station in early April. After it departed, Levi informed June and the Lynches, "The driver said some soldiers had deserted from Leavenworth. Probably got sick of staying in camp during the winter. They've already shot their lieutenant and some sodbusters up the river. It's best to be warned."

Mr. Lynch chided Levi for his pessimism and commented that the army had probably caught the deserters by now. The Lynches' naivete worried June.

Fifteen months of Levi's training plus her own experience had taught June to expect trouble from every quarter. How was it that the Lynches hadn't learned their lessons after what had happened to them during the war?

"They're the types who go around preaching that it's always darkest before the dawn," Levi commented later. "And right now, they think their troubles are over. What they don't realize is that everyone stays in darkness for most of their lives."

The passengers called out their farewells as the coach rumbled west toward the sun. June glanced up at the sky. The sun was unusually bright. That meant there were at least a few hours of daylight left. It was time to begin supper.

June picked up the two buckets and headed toward the river. After she filled one bucket with water, she glanced up and noticed several figures approaching. Nine of them.

Suspicious, June hid behind a tree and peered at the figures for closer inspection. Her heart nearly jolted at the sight of the blue uniforms with facings. There was no doubt they were the army deserters from Leavenworth.

Chapter 7

Lynch's Station, Spring 1867.

The nine men in uniform edged closer to the river. "Hey, Reese!" a deep voice shouted. "There's someone by the river! A skirt, I think!"

Another voice replied, just as deep and with a rasp, "I reckon we'll have us some entertainment this evening, boys! Hey there, girlie! Come on out!"

June's heart beat rapidly as she glanced around for a weapon. *Dammit! Why didn't she have the sense to bring a gun along?* With no weapon, there was only one other recourse.

Hoping to God no one would catch her, June abandoned the buckets, lifted her skirt, and ran as fast as she could. She reached the station within minutes and raised the alarm. Levi immediately took command.

"Miz Lynch, you and June hide in the cellar underneath the stables. I'll make sure to give…."

June cried in protest. "Wait a minute! Why do I have to hide? I can fight just as good as you!"

Levi grabbed her shoulders. "Look girl, I know you can shoot, but I need you to look after the missus."

"But…."

"Dammit, June! There's no time to argue. They got twice the guns we have." A strange light glowed in his dark eyes.

June finally understood. The mountain man was trying to tell her that they had little chance of survival. There was no telling what would happen if the deserters got their hands on the women. Mrs. Lynch let out a cry and clasped her husband. As he escorted the two women to the stable, he tried to comfort her.

Levi swept away some hay and opened a trap door. "In here, ladies." He handed June two of the new Spencer rifles and three revolvers. "If the bastards find you, make sure you get some before they get you."

June glanced at the mountain man and nodded. He smiled and went back upstairs, shutting the trap door behind them. The hole suddenly became dark.

Mrs. Lynch began to whimper.

"Please, ma'am," June hissed. "Be quiet!"

Several minutes passed, June did not know how many, before she heard that raspy voice cry out, "Hey! Anybody here?" When there was no reply, Raspy continued. "You boys, search this place." June's heart beat rapidly.

But the search was halted by Mr. Lynch asking, "How may I help you?"

"What's this place?"

"The Lynch station for the Overland–Pike's Peak Stagecoach Line. My name is Lynch."

A trail of dust filtered into June's nostrils. She had to fight the urge to sneeze.

The voice asked, "Where the others?"

Silence.

"Where the others, old man? You can't be running this place alone! One of my men saw this pretty little darky near the river!" June closed her eyes. "Where is she?"

Mr. Lynch hesitated. "She left. She got frightened and ran off after spotting your men."

"Yeah, right! Now where are the others?"

Again, silence. Both women inside the cellar anxiously awaited Mr. Lynch's reply.

"I...," he began. "I don't know."

"You goddam liar!"

Someone fired a rifle.

Mrs. Lynch gasped. June reached out and managed to cover the woman's lips in time to stifle a scream.

Raspy continued, "Seamus, look around to see if you can find anyone else." June and Mrs. Lynch heard a few footsteps overhead. Someone was inside the stables.

"Look!" one deserter cried. He sounded upset. "It's Toby! Jesus, someone chopped up his insides!"

Good for you, Levi! June crowed silently.

Then more cries. "Hey! Hey! There he is! It's a

nigger! Get him!"

Hell seemed to break loose above. The cries were followed by an exchange of gunfire. The noise continued for several minutes before it stopped.

"I got him, Reese!" a gruff voice shouted. "I got the darky!"

Tears streamed down June's cheeks. She knew that Levi was dead.

Apparently, Reese was the name of the raspy-voiced leader, because he replied, "Good! Look for more! If you find any others, kill 'em! Otherwise take what you can and burn the place!"

The two women remained huddled while the intruders roamed above. Mrs. Lynch began to whimper again, but this time June was too upset to stop her.

At least an hour passed before acrid smoke drifted from above and they realized the station had been set on fire. Both women began to cough.

"June," Mrs. Lynch wheezed, "I can't stand this smoke any longer. I have to get out!"

"OK. Here." June cocked a pistol and gave it to the older woman. "Use it any way you think best." Their eyes met. Mrs. Lynch seemed to understand what she meant.

June felt the trap door for heat. It was still cool. Good. The fire had not reached their part of the stable. She slowly opened it and climbed out. Mrs. Lynch followed.

The entire west wing of the stable had become a fiery inferno. All the horses were gone. Mrs. Lynch drifted toward the stable doors and cried out. June rushed toward her. Mrs. Lynch was staring down at the body of her husband, who was lying on his back with a neat bullet hole in the center of his forehead. Just like Artemus Lake, June thought. The grief-stricken Mrs. Lynch knelt on the ground and wept over her husband's corpse. June left her alone.

She found one deserter behind the stable, his body literally hacked in two and scalped. June's stomach heaved at the sight and she turned away to avoid losing control. Unfortunately her eyes fell on another corpse in uniform. This one had his brains blown out.

Levi's handiwork. It had to be. Mr. Lynch had been killed immediately after the deserters' arrival.

June discovered Levi's body next to the corral, his left leg poking through the fence. Whoever had killed him had fired three times into his body.

Numb with grief, June choked on her tears as she forced the former mountain man's leg from the fence. Tears flowed but she could not cry aloud. She was too sick at heart to do anything.

The two women discovered that the deserters had failed to set fire to Levi's cabin. After burying Levi and Mr. Lynch, June and Mrs. Lynch spent the night inside the cabin. The widow of the station master cried herself to sleep. June's tears had ceased, but it took her much longer to relax and let go of her thoughts.

"June!" Mrs. Lynch's shriek woke her up the next morning.

"Huh?" June was slightly disoriented.

"June! I hear horses! Someone's coming!"

The two rushed out of the cabin, grabbing rifles on their way. The rays of the morning sun lit the grim landscape and the charred ruins of the station, from which columns of smoke still rose. Blue-clad riders were approaching the station.

Nervous over the possibility of more trouble, the two women aimed their rifles at the newcomers. As the horsemen cantered closer, June relaxed. Brown faces, except for one white and one bronzed, rose above the army uniforms. Levi's two victims had been white. One thing she was certain of: the deserters would not have tolerated blacks among them.

"Halt!" the white officer cried. He dismounted and approached the two women. "Lieutenant Gerard Beavin, ma'am," he said to Mrs. Lynch. He was a slender, short man, with curly dark hair and a moustache. "What happened here, ma'am? Indians?"

Mrs. Lynch was speechless. It was June who answered. She retorted sharply, "You see any arrows around, lieutenant? We were attacked by army men!"

The lieutenant frowned at June. "The deserters from Fort Leavenworth?"

"That's right. They killed two men, stole our horses, and burned the place."

The lieutenant paled. After taking a deep breath, he snapped an order to his noncom: "Sergeant!"

June gasped when she recognized the man who dismounted—Charlie Taylor.

Since Mrs. Lynch still appeared to be in shock over the death of her husband, June decided she would have to take responsibility for notifying Levi's sons of the tragedy. With the station gone, the only place she could look for an address was his cabin.

There was not much in the cabin. Only a bed, a table, two chairs, and a few clothes inside a long wooden box, all recently cleaned, thanks to June. A Kentucky rifle stood in the corner to the left of the doorway. June rummaged in the box and found a pouch containing several letters and a few newspaper clippings.

June examined the letters. One from his oldest son was dated eighteen months ago, three months after she had first met Levi.

October 10, 1865

Dear Papa,

I've just received a letter from Josh's partner in Fort Laramie. Josh was shot and injured by a fugitive named Harry Drummond, a stage robber. Josh and Frank Spencer had cornered the killer and two others near the Sweetwater River. During the gunfight, Josh was shot in the side. Another partner, Jemmy Slade, was killed. Drummond's men were killed and the outlaw captured. Frank did not write to you because he had no idea where you were. If you want, we can meet at Laramie to visit Josh. I hope he's still alive. Is there a way we can talk him out of manhunting? See you in Laramie soon.

Your loving son,
Carson

June had forgotten about the son that Levi had told her was a bounty hunter up north. It was a shame he was so far away. If he lived nearby, she might go to him and suggest that the two of them track down the killers together.

"June?" She turned around. Charlie stood behind her, an odd expression on his face. "June, you better come out. We got problems with Miz Lynch."

She asked, "What's wrong?"

"I don't know. She's ranting at the lieutenant about those deserters. She won't listen to reason."

June brushed past the handsome trooper and went outside. Until now Mrs. Lynch's behavior had been almost unnaturally quiet, as if attempting to deny her grief. Now she had gone to the opposite extreme. With her face red and straggles of hair escaping her chignon, she railed at the officer wildly.

"What's going on?" June demanded.

"June! June!" the widow cried, her voice shrill and high-pitched. "This idiot won't follow Nelson and Levi's killers. He's going to take us to Fort Riley instead!"

The fussy lieutenant sighed. It was obvious he found dealing with the two women a chore. "The commander of the deserters' regiment has already sent trackers after them, Mrs. Lynch. I will contact him and inform him that the men are heading west and…."

"What makes you think they're heading west? Have you looked at their tracks?" June asked.

"Please, Miss Daley, it is obvious they have been

moving in a westerly direction since Leavenworth. Where else would they go?"

"How about the Indian Territory? There they don't have to worry about Yankee law! Many outlaws go there!"

A superior smile formed on Lieutenant Beavin's lips. "The Indian Territory is too dangerous. Especially for army men. I doubt very much they will head there."

"Oh? You managed to guess all that without looking at their tracks?"

Upset by June's barb, the lieutenant coldly informed her that it was obvious the deserters would not be so foolish as to enter the Indian Territory.

"Well I checked around yesterday evening, and I found seven sets of tracks heading due south. That's toward Indian country if I'm not mistaken. Now, I don't know about you, but I'm going after them."

"I wouldn't advise that, miss."

"What are you going to do? Stop me?"

Charlie approached, looking very concerned. "June, what on earth is the matter with you? You're acting crazier than Miz Lynch."

"Please, Charlie," June said, "don't start with me as well. Neither you nor that idiot lieutenant can talk me out of this."

"Now, wait a minute, June! Why don't you just listen for a...."

But June would not listen. Before he could finish, she walked away and headed for Levi's cabin. Charlie followed her.

Inside the cabin, she packed most of Levi's possessions in the wooden box to be sent to his son in Wyoming Territory. June kept some of Levi's clothes and rolled them inside a blanket. She needed them because most of her clothes had been burned with the station house.

Back outside, they found Mrs. Lynch sitting forlornly on the ground, nursing a tin cup filled with coffee. A short, thin trooper with dark skin stood behind the widow, holding the reins of two horses, one which June had earlier seen Charlie riding. The other horse was provided for June by a trooper who was now doubled up with another soldier on his mount.

Looking very displeased, the lieutenant strode toward June. "Since I cannot stop you from making this foolhardy trip, Miss Daley, I'm sending Sergeant Taylor to accompany you. You'll need someone to track those men."

"I already know how to track," June replied. "Levi taught me."

"That may be so, but the sergeant here has had experience as well. And it's foolish for anyone, man or woman, to go off in this territory alone. Also, someone needs to be concerned about Mrs. Lynch. I understand she has a son in Nebraska?"

June nodded. "In Grand Island. He has a store there."

"We'll take her as far as Ellsworth and telegraph for her son to come pick her up."

"There's a boardinghouse at Ellsworth where she can stay. It's owned by a Miss Wendell. Oh, and send a telegram to Carson Walker at Fort Laramie. He needs to know about his father."

June went to the widow. The woman had not changed clothes since yesterday's attack. All her belongings had been lost in the fire. Since June had taken charge, Mrs. Lynch's manner had once more become calm. "Miz Lynch," she said. "Miz Lynch, I'm leaving now. I'm gonna find those men who killed Mr. Lynch and Levi."

Tears streamed down the older woman's cheeks. Though she remained silent, she nodded. June gently wiped the tears and planted a light kiss on Mrs. Lynch's forehead.

"You don't have to go with me, Charlie," she said to her friend.

Charlie looked determined. "Like the lieutenant, I think you're being foolish, but I'm accompanying you. You need someone to look after you."

"All right, let's go," June ordered Charlie. "I don't want to lose track of those killers. They already got half-a-day's ride ahead of us."

The two mounted their horses and rode away.

Chapter 8

The Arkansas River, 1867.

June and Charlie headed south and, as they progressed, they picked up some tracks. More were found, including a set June recognized as belonging to Rusty, along the banks of the Arkansas River. There was no doubt that Levi's killers were headed for the Indian Territory as June had suspected.

"I can't believe they're that stupid!" Charlie declared. "Almost no white man is safe down there, whether in uniform or not!"

June replied, "They probably hope to join the outlaws there."

Within four days, June and Charlie reached the outskirts of Wichita, a dismal collection of dilapidated shacks and two-story buildings.

"Hell, this place looks worse than Ellsworth." She

sniffed the air. "And what is that smell?"

Charlie answered, "Cattle. From Texas. They've been shipping them here and to other Kansas towns since the end of the war."

"I've smelled cow manure before," June said, "but it was never like this."

"You probably never came across so much in one place," Charlie said with a laugh.

After arriving in the town, June and Charlie checked with the local marshal to inquire about the deserters. The unfriendly man refused to help and they immediately left.

"He sure was one mean bastard," Charlie commented. "He acted as if he wanted to lock us up instead."

June suggested they set up camp outside the town.

"No money?"

"I've got money," June replied, patting her stomach. Since leaving Denver, she had worn a money belt around her waist. The only times she ever took it off were when she took her baths. "I just don't want to hang around there." The marshal's reception and the cold stares from the locals had convinced her it would be best not to stay around town.

They left Wichita and set up camp fifteen miles south of the town. Stars sparkled like diamonds in the dark sky. The delicious roast quail contributed to June's drowsy state. She fell asleep within minutes after settling underneath her bedroll.

Then her dream started. June was back at the stage station. Again the deserters attacked, only they were being led by Harlin. After Levi and Mr. Lynch were killed, the rogue army troopers discovered her and Mrs. Lynch where they were hiding, in the hole underneath the stable. Harlin dragged her out first and, with a flourish, brandished a sharp knife. He was about to strike when June woke up with a cry.

Charlie woke up and grabbed for his gun. "What is it?" He stared at June with bleary eyes. "You okay, June?"

"I…uh…," June began. She could not utter another word. The young woman looked about her, feeling frightened and alone. She then began to sob. Charlie sat up and gently gathered her into his arms.

"It's okay, honey," he murmured. "It's okay." Quietly the two rocked back and forth until June lifted her head and kissed his lips. "What?" Charlie looked surprised.

"Please, Charlie," June said softly. She needed him very much. Inside her if possible. "Just for tonight?" She kissed him harder and the trooper returned the kiss. They slowly undressed and slid under his bedroll. Quickly their bodies became entwined.

They were back on the trail the next morning. Neither June nor Charlie commented on what had happened the preceding night, though it was obvious from Charlie's expression that he wanted to.

June's thoughts had once again returned to the deserters. She and Charlie had lost track of their prey for several hours. Then Charlie picked it up again, ten miles south of the Indian Territory border.

"Looks like they spent the night here," he commented. He and June surveyed the circle of rocks and burnt kindling. The afternoon sun shone brightly. "I reckon they're half a day ahead of us. We might catch up by tomorrow."

June smiled at Charlie, and he smiled back. Memories of their night together assailed her. He had turned out to be quite a surprise for one so straitlaced. June had feared she would shock him with some of the techniques she had learned at the Southern Cross, but Charlie had already known them and a few others unfamiliar to her.

"What are you smiling about?" he asked.

June replied saucily, "It wouldn't be hard for you to guess, I reckon, now would it?" She almost laughed when, to her surprise, the trooper blushed.

The Arkansas River spilled into a large body of water called Lake Kaw. June knew of it from the tales Levi had told of his youth. As she and Charlie continued to follow the river, a putrid odor caught her attention. It smelled like overcooked spoiled meat. In the distance, a column of gray smoke spiraled up in the horizon. They were curious about the smoke and the smell, but it was off their route, so they did not take time to investigate.

Fifteen miles later, the pair came upon a wide, one-story cabin with a porch. A blue-clad soldier paced back and forth, armed with a rifle. "Whiskey ranch," Charlie commented. They hid themselves in a deep hollow. Several horses were hitched to the post out front—including Rusty, June noted. "Probably some trader or an Indian agent selling guns, whiskey, and other goods to the Indians. They're a scourge to the army."

"Why?" June asked. "'Cause they sell guns to the Indians?"

"Yep." Charlie did not catch her sarcasm. "Especially whiskey. You don't wanna meet a drunken Indian."

"I reckon I wouldn't want to meet with a drunken white man either. Or colored." Charlie glanced at June sharply. "That stuff about Indians and whiskey is a lot of bunk. Levi told me that whites can't hold their liquor any better, and they drink twice as much."

Charlie's lips pressed tightly together in disapproval. He seemed not to care for June's opinion. *Was he always like this whenever someone proved him or his precious army wrong?* June hoped not. She had no patience with an opinionated man. Even if she did liked him.

June sighed. She turned her head around and froze at the sight of three men astride horses. The calico shirts, buckskin trousers, the braids underneath the wide-brimmed hats, and the bronze-colored skin identified them as Indians.

"Charlie," she said quietly, "look behind you and keep calm."

Charlie peeked over his shoulder. "Oh, Jesus!" he whispered fiercely. "Where the hell did they come from?"

"I don't know. I doubt if they're from a Plains tribe, though. Looks like Indian police." June raised her arm

121

in a greeting.

The three men returned the gesture. They quickly dismounted from their horses and scrambled toward the couple. One of them, a tall, slender fellow with narrow features and a rock-hard frame, knelt beside June.

"Joe Redfeather. With the Cherokee Nation. Indian police," he said, holding out his hand. June shook it. She introduced herself and Charlie.

"Those two are Ned Gray Cloud and Bobby Sixfoot. What are you two doing here?"

Charlie answered, "Looking for army deserters. They wiped out a stagecoach station back in Kansas."

"And the army sent you to find them?" The Cherokee lifted his left eyebrow in a sardonic manner.

Charlie blushed and stammered. June explained: "Not exactly. I was going after them on my own. They killed two friends of mine. Since the army couldn't talk me out of it, they sent him," she nodded toward Charlie, "to help me."

Joe Redfeather explained that he and his men had discovered dead bodies and burnt ruins at a Cherokee ranch near Lake Kaw. They had traced the perpetrators to the whiskey station. He examined Charlie more closely. "So you're a pony soldier, eh?"

Charlie hesitated for a moment before finally acknowledging the fact.

"Well, at least you don't have Win Hancock behind you."

Charlie ignored the gibe and asked, "How are we

going to get those boys in there?"

Everyone became quiet. A jaybird's sharp cry and laughter from inside the cabin interrupted the silence. June finally spoke up. "If you all don't mind listening to a woman, I reckon I got a plan." The men stared at her. "First, what we need is a knife. Or bow-and-arrow if anyone has one."

Ned Gray Cloud, a short, stocky Cherokee with unusually pale gray eyes, withdrew a sharp knife. Quietly, he stalked toward the sentry until he was right behind him. Gray Cloud plunged the knife into the blue uniform, killing the deserter instantly.

Boldly, June walked up to the station's porch and knocked on the door. "Anybody there?" she called out. The laughter halted. She heard a few clicks. "Hello? Somebody better come out real quick! There's a dead man out here!"

Several men rushed out of the cabin with rifles in their hands. The deserters. Two of them still wore army coats. One was a large man with a red beard. He stared first at her, and then at the body of the sentry.

"What the hell?" he cried in a raspy voice, which June instantly recognized as that of the leader of the deserters. "Who the hell are you?"

Before June could open her mouth, one of his men shouted, "Hey, Reese! Carter's body is still warm! He ain't even been dead two minutes!"

Reese grabbed June, taking her by surprise. "All right! Just who in the hell are you?"

"Your maker, you murdering bastard!"

Surprised by June's answer, Reese made the mistake of releasing her arm. Too late the trooper reached for his gun. Being swifter, June withdrew hers and shot Reese in the chest.

Another trooper aimed his rifle at her before he was shot down. By whom June did not know.

A gun battle followed. June ducked to avoid the flying bullets. She then ran inside the building, where she discovered a tall, lanky trooper—one of the deserters—with his gun aimed at a long-haired man behind the makeshift counter, obviously the owner of the ranch. June shot the deserter in the back.

She sensed someone behind her and whirled around. One of the Cherokee policemen, Bobby Sixfoot, stood in the doorway. Her body sagged with relief. "Thank God! I thought...."

"Look out!" the Cherokee cried. June's eyes fell upon another deserter in the far corner of the cabin, his rifle aimed at her head. At the sound of a shot, she jumped. But it was not the deserter who had fired. Sixfoot had just blown open the trooper's head with a shotgun.

Shaking as if she had palsy, June leaned against the counter and sighed with relief. "Thanks, Mr. Sixfoot," she said.

The Cherokee lawman nodded.

Another five minutes passed before the last gunshot was heard from outside. The long-haired owner of the ranch peeked outside. "Hey, it's over!" he cried. "I think your friends got them all!"

June and Sixfoot rushed outside and discovered five bodies scattered about the grounds. None of them belonged to the group who had staged the attack.

At first, June was delighted by the fact that all of the men responsible for Levi's death had been killed, but then the realization hit her: she had killed two men in less than five minutes. Nausea rising in her throat, she raced behind the building and threw up.

"June?" Charlie found her leaning against the cabin wall, her eyes closed. "You feeling all right?"

"I'm fine. Just got a little sick, that's all."

"Are you sure?"

"Dammit, Charlie! I said I was fine!" Sometimes she wished he would stop treating her like some fragile piece of china!

The young trooper looked away. *Now, why did I do that?* June thought. The poor boy was just concerned about me. "I'm fine," she said in a more subdued tone. "What is it?"

"The rest of us took care of those boys out front," Charlie said.

"That's seven of 'em we'll have to take back to Kansas," June said.

"How on earth are we gonna drag seven bodies back? And why should we?"

"How else am I gonna collect the bounty on them? I need proof."

"The bounty? I thought you wanted to go after these boys for revenge."

"I did. but I don't see no harm in collecting any bounty on them as well." While Charlie stared at her with dismay, June glanced up. Her gaze fell upon a wagon parked a few yards away, next to a cottonwood tree. "There," she said, pointing to it. "I reckon our little problem is now solved."

The owner of the station was a Mr. Hiram Mercer, formerly of Springfield, Illinois. He was more than happy to sell June the wagon. "Anything to get those bastards out of my sight," he said. "In fact, you can have it free. Hell, they were about to rob me blind. After what your friends did today, I reckon I wouldn't mind you having it."

Mr. Mercer served the party a meal of venison stew, sourdough biscuits, and coffee before they started on their way. He also offered them whiskey as a parting gift. Only Charlie and Bobby Sixfoot took up the offer.

After the meal, June and Charlie hitched the two army horses to the wagon. As the trooper climbed aboard the seat, June tied Rusty to the back of the wagon and joined Charlie. The couple and the three Cherokees then bid Mr. Mercer good-bye before riding away.

June and Charlie followed the Cherokees to their village, a pleasant-looking settlement that resembled the towns in Kansas and Nebraska. June was surprised to find not only red but also black citizens roaming the streets. At the police station, she and Charlie gave statements on the recent gunfight. "If there's any reward for those boys," Charlie told the Cherokees, "I'll make sure the army finds out about your help."

"That's all right," said Redfeather. "We got what

we wanted—the men who burned that ranch. It belonged to one of our people, a Sam Ross. His wife and daughter were raped before being killed. Then those dogs beat poor Sam to death before burning him. Just make sure the army keeps others like them away. Huh?" He said the last remark with his usual cynicism.

June wondered if Joe Redfeather was referring to the recent army troop movements in the territory against the southern Cheyenne.

She and Charlie both bid their former companions good-bye and returned north to Kansas with seven dead bodies in a wagon.

June and Charlie reached Ellsworth the second week of May, and they found a surprise awaiting them inside the parlor at Miss Wendell's boardinghouse. June had no idea who the white man was, but the black man looked very familiar, though she could not immediately place the face.

"Josh Walker?" Charlie declared loudly. "What are you doing here?"

So this was Levi's younger son, the bounty hunter. June examined him. He looked the way Levi must have done nearly a quarter of a century ago. Like his father, he was tall, with intense dark eyes that seemed to bore right through you. The only difference was the cheekbones he had inherited from his mother. Sharp as a knife they were.

"Charlie," Walker replied. Though he shook the trooper's hand, he did not seemed thrilled to see him.

"You remember Frank Spencer, my partner?" He indicated the white man standing beside him. "We came here to pick up Pa's body."

Charlie nodded at Spencer coolly. "This is June Daley. She worked at the way station with Levi. June, this is Josh Walker, Levi's...."

"Levi's son." June shook the young man's hand. He had a nice, strong grip. And his quiet demeanor seemed to enhance his good looks. The two pairs of eyes met. June felt as if a shaft had pierced through her very soul. "Nice to meet you finally."

Josh glanced outside the window. "Same here. I saw the wagon you arrived in. I reckon you've delivered those boys who killed my pa?"

June nodded. She did not tell him that she and Charlie had each received a three-hundred-dollar reward for the return of the deserters. A strained silence enveloped the room.

"I reckon we best be on our way, Josh," his partner said, breaking the silence. The southern accent struck a familiar chord in June.

She turned to Mr. Spencer. He was just as tall as Josh, with a square, handsome face and dark brown hair. "Are you by any chance from Tennessee or Georgia?"

"Georgia, miss." His southern accent was slightly refined. "My family's place lies between Atlanta and Savannah." Curious blue eyes examined her. "You from Tennessee?"

June nodded.

"Thought so. My mama's family lives near

Memphis."

"Where are you taking Levi?"

Joshua answered, "Back to Wyoming. For burial."

"Mind if I come along?"

Charlie and Joshua stared at her in surprise. Charlie seemed especially taken aback by her request. "You're leaving Kansas?"

Oblivious to the stares the two bounty hunters were directing toward her and Charlie, June blushed. "I want to pay my last respects to Levi." She turned to the other two. "When are you leaving?"

"In about an hour," Josh answered. "If you're coming with us, you can meet us outside."

June nodded as the bounty hunters left the parlor.

"How long will you be gone?" Charlie asked as soon as they were alone.

"Probably only for a few days. After that, I'm heading back to Denver."

"Wait a minute! I thought you were planning to hang around Kansas, looking for what's-his-name?"

"Harlin. And I haven't forgotten him. In fact, I don't think he's around here anymore. There hasn't been any news. And the marshal told me he and his boys had been seen in Colorado again."

Charlie took hold of June's hand and began to caress it. Those passionate nights on the trail suddenly reappeared in June's thoughts. "Charlie…."

"I…I was hoping you'd stay here in Kansas. With me perhaps. And be my wife?" Charlie gazed at her hopefully.

June felt a sudden tug at her heart. Unable to meet

his eyes because of what she was about to do, she lowered her eyes. "Charlie," she said softly. "You're a good man and all, but...."

"But what?"

"There's still Harlin to look for...."

Charlie let out a brief curse, breaking the tender moment.

June finished more boldly. "And I don't want to be an army wife. After that night near Wichita, I tried to imagine myself as one and couldn't. I'd hate it. I know I would. Now, if you were to leave...."

For the third time, Charlie interrupted. "I can't do that, June! The army's my life." The hazel eyes that met June's were cold and hard. "But I can see it ain't yours. Good-bye."

"Charlie!"

It was too late. The trooper was already leaving the parlor, and he refused to turn back. June had expected to feel sad at parting with Charlie. Instead, she felt nothing except relief. Perhaps Levi had been right after all. Perhaps Charlie wasn't the man for her.

Chapter 9

Walker Ranch, Wyoming Territory, June 1867.

Four men lowed the coffin into the freshly dug hole in the ground. A tall young man with reddish-brown skin murmured final prayers, sprinkled dust on the coffin, and finished the ceremony with a quiet "Amen." Levi Walker was finally put to rest.

Along with June, Josh Walker, and Frank Spencer, several of the Wyoming neighbors stood about the graveside in somber silence. Kansas was not the only place where Levi had been known and liked, it seemed. Even the remaining family of the rancher's former Cheyenne wife came to pay last respects.

The young man who had conducted the service was Levi's older son, Carson. Like Josh, he strongly resembled his father. The difference between them was that Carson did not have Josh's high cheekbones and intense black eyes. Standing alongside Carson was his wife, a young woman of twenty-five, whose skin was lighter than either of the two brothers.

Everyone went back to the one-story ranch house for food and drinks. Several people asked June about her relationship with Levi. She repeated the story she had earlier told Josh and Frank about her employment at Lynch's station, the deserters' attack, Levi's death, and her final showdown with his killers at the whiskey ranch in the Indian Territory.

She didn't mention the stop she had made in the Nebraska Territory, where she had visited Mrs. Lynch at her son's house. According to the son, the widow hardly ever talked with anyone and stayed upstairs in her bedroom. But she welcomed June's visit.

June suddenly recalled the tears of relief that rolled down that ravaged face when she heard about the deaths of her husband's killers. June shivered and brushed away the haunting memory.

"Something wrong, Miss Daley?" Carson asked, a concerned expression on his face.

June smiled. "No, I was just thinking about poor Mrs. Lynch."

"My father wrote to me about her and Mr. Lynch. I think I feel even more sorry for her than for him." Carson turned his attention to other matters. "By the way, my brother tells me you're heading back for Denver. What do you plan to do there?"

June answered, "Find a place to live first, and then perhaps a job."

"I hope you have luck finding one," Carson's wife

remarked. "With the city still growing, it shouldn't be too hard. I remember when Denver was first founded and...."

The petite woman went on talking about the early days in Denver, before the war. June did not know what to make of Levi's daughter-in-law. She did not strike June as the type who could withstand frontier living. Levi had once mentioned that Diane came from New York with her family during Denver's first gold rush. The young woman's origins did not come as much of a surprise to June. She seemed to belong more to the parlors back east than to the frontier.

The next morning, June prepared to return to Denver. Anxious to hit the trail, she wanted to leave right after breakfast. Immediately after finishing her meal, she left for the stable to pack her bedroll and saddle Rusty. Then, going back into the kitchen, she said good-bye to Levi's family.

Josh and Frank stood up. "Miss Daley," said Josh. "Could we speak to you for a minute? Outside?"

"Sure." June was surprised. She wondered what the pair wanted, but she followed them back to the stable. "What is it you want?" she asked.

Josh nervously cleared his throat. "Just before he died, Pa wrote to tell me about your search for Harlin Mason."

June stared at him.

"He said you were hoping that Artemus Lake would help," Josh continued. "But since he's dead, Frank and I thought maybe we could."

"That's a mean bunch Mason rides with, Miss

133

Daley," Frank added. Unlike Josh, who seemed mild-mannered, the Georgian was a more direct man. "They're already wanted in three different territories for some unspeakable crimes. Josh and I realize you've been down in the Indian Territory and all, but Harlin Mason and Ben Carlson are real bastards. Neither Josh or I would go after them alone. And you being a...."

"A woman?" June added. Her eyes glittered with challenge. "You don't think I can handle myself?"

Josh spoke more firmly. "I'm sure you can, miss. But like Frank said, Harlin Mason and Ben Carlson are not the kind of men anyone should go after alone. We were hoping you would want us to join you. We've got time on our hands."

June realized the two meant well and regretted her assumption that they considered her incapable of being a bounty hunter. Truthfully, she had planned to ask for their help, but that had been before her trip to the Indian Territory—before she had discovered that she might have a talent for the business herself.

Her tone softened. "Thanks, boys. It's gonna be awhile before I can even start searching for Harlin. But if I ever need help, I'll let you know."

The two men glanced at each other and shrugged. Frank took her hand and shook it. "Good luck, miss," he said and left the stable.

Josh remained facing June. It was hard for her to keep from staring at those magnetic black eyes. "If you do need any help," he said, "just leave a message for me or Frank at Fort Laramie. We usually hang around there between jobs."

June smiled. "I'll do that. Thanks for your help." She stuck out her hand. Josh shook it. "Well, good-bye."

"So long. Take care of yourself."

June mounted Rusty. For no particular reason, she turned around in her saddle and noticed that Josh had not moved but remained in the same spot, staring at her. She gave him one last wave and rode away. As she passed through the gateway, a chill ran through her.

Denver had not changed much in a year and a half. It still had not grown into a bustling boomtown like San Francisco, despite the continual stream of gold. Remembering Tim McPherson's complaints of his difficulties in reaching the veins, June figured that not enough gold was coming in. Cattle was Denver's first industry, cattle from the ranches established in the valleys outside the city.

To June, the city resembled a large version of the Kansas cow towns. She watched a herd of cattle ramble down Fourteenth Street. The bellowing bulls weaved past teamster wagons, horsemen, and emigrant wagons. June wrinkled her nose as one bull stopped in the middle of the street and released a pile of waste on the ground. Lord, those creatures smelled awful! And poor old Denver would have to endure this until the end of the summer.

It did not take June very long to reach the site of the Southern Cross saloon, but the sign above the swing doors now read: "MacKenna's Saloon." What had happened to Allen Cross and Therese Aubry?

The white frame house looked the same as ever. June recognized two figures hanging a sign above the door—Clarice and Leanne.

"Hey! You two!" June cried. "Look who's here!" Leanne, who was standing on a ladder, slipped and almost fell before Clarice caught her.

Both women's mouths opened with surprise. Then they cried at once. "June! You crazy woman! What the hell are you doing here?"

June replied, after hugging her friends, "I could ask you what the hell is going on with this place? Who's MacKenna?" She pointed at the saloon.

Clarice replied, "He's the new owner. Bought it from the city after Mister Allen and Miz Therese decided to leave."

"And how did this miracle come about?"

The two prostitutes explained that Cross and Therese had come into conflict with a new city official three months ago. After threatening the man and trying to bribe him, the two owners had been kicked out of town and their property seized.

Leanne continued, "Some fella named MacKenna bought the saloon. Me an Clarice bought the house. We'll be opening up in two weeks." The blonde woman cocked a mischievous brow. "You want to join us?"

June barked a short laugh. "No disrespect to you girls, but working in a cathouse was never my ambition. Besides, I got better things to do." She started for her horse. "Is Tim McPherson still around?"

Clarice told her that the miner still lived in the same place. "Found himself a new vein of gold last year. Reckon he's been using some of that money to find his brother's killer. He's already hired four bounty hunters." She added, "Course, he ain't been around here lately. Found himself a woman, the sly dog. Turns out she's an old friend of ours. Listen, we're gonna be busy today, but why don't you come around sometime? Maybe for supper?"

June accepted. "Maybe at the end of the week. I'll see you."

Her next stop was Tim McPherson's home. "Well, well! Look who's come back!" the mine owner greeted her with a hug. "I was beginning to wonder if I would ever hear from you again. You haven't written since February."

June said, "A lot has happened since then. Why don't you let me in and I'll tell you."

After recounting her adventures in the Indian Territory, June told Tim her plans. He nearly choked on his cigar.

"You're still trying to go after Mason? Are you crazy?"

June frowned, annoyed by his reaction. "Why not? Look how I helped track those army boys in the Indian Territory! I never said it would be easy, but damn! At least give me a chance to prove myself!"

Looking like a frustrated rooster, Tim squirmed about in his seat. "Dammit, June! Didn't we go through this before? I told you that you need to know the land around here!"

"I know Colorado and Kansas and the Indian Territory. That's good enough for a start."

"For a st...!"

"And don't tell me it's a waste of my time looking for Harlin! You want him caught as badly as I do! I've heard about those bounty hunters you've sent after him."

"They were experienced professionals!"

"And have they found him?"

"All right! None of them have found him or those friends of his since Bert Todd's death. What makes you think you can?"

June's eyes left Tim's face. "I might have better luck," she murmured.

Tim snorted. "Yeah, right." He leaned back into his chair and sighed. "I can't talk you out of this, can I?"

"No."

"I thought so." Another sigh. "Jesus, you are the most stubborn woman I've ever met. I shouldn't be surprised if you do find him."

June smiled. "Thanks, Tim."

Now that she was back in Denver, June needed a permanent home. Tim told her about a former prostitute who was running a boardinghouse near Cherry Creek. She was the new woman in his life whom Clarice had mentioned.

"Her name's Carrie Jackson," Tim said. "She used to work at the Southern Cross like you, until she married one of her customers. The old boy dropped dead on her about a year ago."

The boardinghouse was a three-story building just two blocks away from Cherry Creek. June liked it the moment she laid eyes on it. Quiet, remote and obviously respectable. Its owner was a tall brunette with a husky voice. She eyed June from across the table inside the parlor with magnetic midnight blue eyes. No wonder Tim was so smitten!

"So you used to work at the Southern Cross, huh?" Mrs. Jackson—or Carrie, as she liked to be called—said.

June nodded. She wished Tim had not mentioned anything about the cathouse.

"I never thought I'd see the day I would meet another soul who escaped that perfumed rat trap! Welcome to the Jackson House." Carrie took June's hand and shook it. The younger woman sighed with relief.

"Thanks. How did you get out?" June asked.

"My late husband proposed marriage to me. Actually, I would have preferred if Tim had asked me, but he wasn't ready then. Still, Cornelius was a good husband. He had to pay Cross and Therese three thousand to get me out of there." The landlady handed June a glass of lemonade. "How about you?"

"Two thousand dollars and a .44 Allen pepperbox. The last was used to keep Jimmy Morrow's fists away from my face."

Carrie broke into a rich laugh. "Hell, I could just see Jimmy's face when you pulled that gun on him. I wouldn't be surprised if he wet himself."

The image of the hulkish lout wetting his pants prompted June to join in the older woman's laughter. A new home at last.

June's first act in establishing her new profession was a trip to the marshal's office the next day. Except for a handyman, the front office was empty. June examined the bulletin board, which was covered with wanted posters. Harlin's likeness still remained on the board, along with the other members of his gang. The gang's last known whereabouts had been at a Julesburg bank, nearly a year ago. June cursed silently. Then a picture of a round face with narrow eyes and whiskers caught her attention. The inscription below read:

WANTED!
PHIL O'KEEFE

for the murder of NATHANIEL McPHERSON, October 16, 1865; the robbery of the Julesburg Bank on August 3, 1866; the murders of Jonathan and Dora Sanderson in Arapahoe County on February 20, 1867; and robbery of the La Junta Commerce Bank on June 10, 1867. Rode with Bert Todd, Harlin Mason, Ben Carlson, Adam Jenkins, and Barney Ward. Wanted alone for the Sanderson murders and the La Junta bank robbery. $5,000.00 Reward for his capture.

Signed
Territorial Govenor

So Phil O'Keefe was last seen in La Junta just two weeks ago. Interesting. That meant his trail was still fresh enough to trace—a trail that just might lead her to Harlin.

The next morning she saddled Rusty, said good-bye to Carrie and Tim, and headed south for La Junta. Before leaving, Tim had given her a map for her to use on the trip to La Junta. "Be a hell of a lot better than you roaming all over the territory lost."

June had smiled thinly.

It took her a week to reach the small town east of the Sangre de Cristo Mountains.

The town marshal there proved to be as uncooperative as the one June and Charlie had encountered in Kansas. It was obvious he did not take a Negro female bounty hunter seriously. Fortunately for June, she discovered she did not need him. There was someone else who had valuable information on O'Keefe.

Hezekial Jones was a blacksmith with a penchant for the town's news. He knew everyone and everything that occurred. Before the bank was robbed, he had overheard O'Keefe talking to one of the local whores, Maggie Klune, about a hideout.

The blacksmith mentioned this tidbit to the marshal, but he had been unwilling to follow the lead. It turned out the marshal was a regular customer of this Maggie Klune and feared his visits would reach the ears of his wife.

June was pleased that the blacksmith was willing to tell her this. She gave him some gold pieces and asked him to look at Rusty's hooves. "Maggie Klune, huh?"

"That's right," the blacksmith replied. "She's got her own place, two buildings west of the livery stable."

"Thanks." June glanced at her pocketwatch. Three-fifty in the afternoon. There was still time to visit the prostitute before business hours began. As June started across the plaza, she tried to think of a way to approach Miss Klune, since introducing herself as a bounty hunter was out of the question. She decided to say that she was a friend of Harlin's.

The prostitute's house was a dilapidated one-story adobe cottage, surrounded by a fence and weeds in the yard. June had never seen an adobe before, being used to houses and cabins made from wood, brick, or sod. Maggie Klune seemed unconcerned about keeping appearances.

June knocked. A half-dressed woman with stringy brown hair and a puffy face opened the door. She looked half-asleep.

"We're closed," she said brusquely, before June could speak. Her voice was hoarse from too much whiskey. She started to close the door.

June stuck her foot through the opening. "I'm not a customer, Miss Klune. My name's June Daley. I'm a friend of Harlin's."

"Harlin Mason?"

"Yeah. We knew each other back in Tennessee. Harlin and I ran into each other in Nebraska some time ago. He asked me to deliver something for a Phil

O'Keefe." June held up a large bag of coins.

The prostitute's lethargy suddenly disappeared. "So Harlin and Ben finally decided to give Phil his share of the McPherson job."

"That's right." June wondered what Maggie meant. Had Harlin and his cronies not divided the McPherson gold? "Harlin wanted me to say he was sorry it took so long but…."

"Yeah, I know, Colorado ain't safe these days. Too bad Phil didn't have the sense to stay out himself. You can hand me the money; I'll give it to him."

June hesitated.

"Oh, I see," Maggie continued sarcastically. "Harlin wanted you to give it to him personally."

"You can take me to Phil," June replied.

Maggie yawned. "Sorry, honey. Right now, I need all the rest I can get. I'll be working in a few hours. You can find Phil yourself. He's got a little shack just north of here, on the other side of the Arkansas, six miles upriver from the old Bent's Fort."

"Thanks for your…," June began.

"Yeah, right. See ya." The whore closed the door before June could finish. The bitch! she thought nastily. The Southern Cross never would have considered a dirty creature like that to join its stable. Phil O'Keefe could have done better for himself.

Following the woman's directions, June reached Bent's Fort, or at least the burnt remains of what had been the fort. Built in the early 1830s by two brothers, William and Charles Bent, it had served primarily as a post along the old Santa Fe Trail. Levi had

143

told her of his experiences here, including the fact that this had been where he had met his Cheyenne wife, Morning Sun.

After leaving the fort, it was not difficult to find O'Keefe's camp—a little one-story affair made of adobe. The hut was located several yards above the Arkansas River.

As June approached, O'Keefe was outside the hut, chopping wood. He was a short, skinny man with wiry arms and a half-shaven chin. From the looks of him, June figured he could use a bath.

"O'Keefe?" she called out. "You Phil O'Keefe?"

The outlaw dropped his ax and whirled around. As if by magic, a revolver appeared in his hand. June blinked. She decided this fellow might be hard to take.

"Who the hell are you?" he growled, a slight Irish brogue evident in his speech. His gray eyes narrowed.

June smiled in her most disarming manner. "Howdy, the name's June Daley. I'm friend of Harlin Mason."

"So?"

"He sent me to give you a message. I'm to tell you that he and Ben finally got the McPherson gold. They're waiting for you in Nebraska."

O'Keefe stepped closer toward her, eyes suspicious. Nervously, June held her breath.

"Nearly two years I've been waiting for that gold. So Harlin and Ben finally discovered where Bert hid it?"

"Uh, that's right." *So it was Bert Todd who hid the gold.*

"Have they told Adam yet?"

June assumed he meant Adam Jenkins, another member of the gang.

"Harlin's on his way to meet Adam."

O'Keefe took June by surprise by jumping in the air with a loud whoop. "Hot damn! Finally I'm gonna have me some real money!"

O'Keefe continued to carry on while June glanced about the camp. Not much to look at. The hut was a hovel compared to Maggie Klune's house. The river was the best feature around here.

As her eyes returned to the outlaw, June found him observing her in an odd manner. She knew that look very well. "What is it?"

A slow smile crept across O'Keefe's face. "I was thinking this might be the perfect time for a grand celebration. The horizontal kind."

"Oh? What about Harlin?" she asked apprehensively. "What about that girl of yours in La Junta? What's her name, Maggie?"

"What about them? They don't need to know."

O'Keefe stepped forward toward her, and a hollow feeling spread through June's stomach. It had been almost two years since she had left the Southern Cross. She never thought she would have to do this again. If she played her hand right, maybe she wouldn't have to go too far.

June took a deep breath and started to unbutton her calico blouse. "Well, why don't we get started then?" she said.

The outlaw suddenly grabbed June and pulled her

to him roughly, startling her and causing her to gasp. He kissed her mouth hungrily, and his breath smelled of tobacco and whiskey. O'Keefe's hands ripped open her blouse and he nuzzled the flesh above her bodice. Slowly, June slid her right hand toward the gun in his holster.

The revolver firmly in her hand, June raised it and suddenly brought the butt down upon the outlaw's skull, knocking him out cold.

June replaced her ripped blouse with another one from her saddlebag. She then began the arduous task of getting O'Keefe tied up on his horse. It took her nearly thirty minutes. By that time, the outlaw lay belly flat on the saddle, with his hands tied and his feet shackled under the horse's flank. When that was all accomplished, June rested briefly and then started back for Denver, leading her captive's horse.

O'Keefe was something of a nuisance during the trip to Denver. Especially after June attempted to get information on Harlin's whereabouts.

"How in the hell would I know, you cold-hearted bitch?" the outlaw cried. "I'd cut me tongue out before I'd tell you anything!" Although she was allowing him to walk behind the horse by this time, his hands remained tied. She dared not unbind him for fear he would try to kill her and escape.

"Where were you supposed to meet for the next job?" June demanded.

"None of your damned business!"

June smoldered. *Son of a bitch! The bastard was not going to cooperate*. She sighed. Finding Harlin was going to be very difficult. Oh well. At least the five thousand dollars for O'Keefe would soften the disappointment she felt.

Denver was all agog by the news that a novice bounty hunter—a female at that—had ridden into town with Phil O'Keefe as a prisoner. Tim McPherson and Carrie Jackson were stunned.

"I can't believe it!" Tim declared. "I just can't believe it!" He, June, and Carrie were inside Carrie's parlor sipping drinks.

June shrugged. "Go have a look for yourself if you need proof. O'Keefe's sitting in the county jail right now."

Carrie handed her a glass of lemonade. "What are you going to do next?" she asked.

"Check the sheriff's and the marshal's offices for more bounties. See if I can figure out where any more of Harlin's friends might be. Or Harlin himself."

"Won't it take you awhile to find them?"

June allowed herself a wry smile. "Hell, considering how long I've been after Harlin, I reckon I can be patient."

Chapter 10

Denver, Colorado Territory, 1867.

Patience had never been one of June's strong suits, but it was a trait she managed to develop over the following year. Because of her success in capturing O'Keefe, she quickly acquired a reputation as a bounty hunter, and that helped her in tracking down and taking more outlaws. Even though her new profession kept her busy, she was always alert for news of Harlin or his gang.

Phil O'Keefe died at the end of a hangman's noose three months after his capture. That left Ben Carlson, Adam Jenkins, and a thug who had recently joined the gang, Barney Ward, as possible leads to Harlin himself.

Since O'Keefe's death, Harlin and his friends had surfaced six times to commit crimes. These had included three stagecoach robberies in Colorado during the summer of 1867, horse rustling and destruction of a ranch in the New Mexico Territory later that fall, and then they had come back to Colorado for two bank robberies the following spring.

Finally in May, June got a lead on the whereabouts of Adam Jenkins. A former slave from Kentucky, Jenkins was believed to be somewhere near Fort Kearney. When she reached the Nebraska town, June learned that another pair of bounty hunters had arrived ahead of her and had already caught Jenkins. The two were Josh Walker and Frank Spencer. Two days before she got there, Jenkins had been hanged by a lynch mob. Frustrated, June was forced to cool her heels for a night before returning to Colorado.

Luck finally came June's way one hot day in July 1868. She had caught a horse thief not far from Trinidad, and he turned out to be one of Harlin's friends—Barney Ward.

As soon as she discovered his identity she began to ask Ward where Harlin was. Receiving no answers from Ward after persistent questioning, she decided to resort to more persuasive methods. After June shot off his left earlobe, Ward completely broke down and became a blubbering idiot.

"Now, say that again!" June demanded harshly. "Where's Harlin?"

Bleeding profusely from the wound, Ward cried out, "Fool's Gold! It's a mining town south of Denver! At a place call Fields Hotel. That's where we're supposed to meet."

Harlin was back in Colorado. Again. This was the fourth time since Nate Pearson's death in '65 that he and his friends had entered the territory that wanted them desperately. "Why?" she asked Ward.

"I don't know why they keep coming back."

June swung up her arm in a threatening manner.

"I swear! I've only been with them for a little over a year. I reckon they're looking for some lost money or something."

The McPherson gold! June thought triumphantly. It had to be! She remembered O'Keefe mentioning that Bert Todd had hidden the gold. But how could they know where it was? Todd had been dead for nearly three years.

It didn't matter, she decided. As soon as this fool was turned over to the law in Trinidad, Fool's Gold would be June's next stop.

June learned from Trinidad's town marshal that Fool's Gold was eighty-eight miles southwest of Denver. As she traveled toward the Rocky Mountain foothills, she could not help but admire the breathtaking scenery around her. The rocky terrain was somewhat difficult on Rusty, yet June managed to enjoy the green pine trees, boulders, and cool air. It was a refreshing change after years of the brown flatlands of Kansas and eastern Colorado.

June entered the town limits of Fool's Gold six days after leaving Trinidad. One look at the mining community assured her that, once the gold ran out, this place would not last two hours. Fool's Gold was nothing but a collection of wooden shacks, tents, and ramshackle buildings with false fronts, the usual western town. However, the soaring Rocky Mountains in the distance provided a majestic contrast to the eyesore community.

After walking down the muddy street (it had rained just two days before), June finally came upon a wide and surprisingly attractive-looking two-story frame building. Lace curtains were in the window. A red and gold sign hung above the door stating: "Fields Hotel and Parlor."

The plump, matronly woman named Mattie Fields was not June's idea of the owner of a hotel where Harlin might stay. Not this sweet-looking creature with a twinkle in her blue eyes and a cheerful disposition. Either Ward had lied or made a mistake.

"May I help you, my dear?" The woman asked in a soothing voice.

My dear? June was at loss for words for a moment. "Uh, yes, I want a room for the night."

"Of course, dear. That'll be two dollars." Before she could retrieve her money, June caught sight of a half-dressed woman and a grizzled miner heading toward the stairs. "We like to provide a little extra entertainment for some of our customers," Miss Fields added.

June understood what the extra entertainment was. This place was not only a hotel but a whorehouse as well. She stared at the middle-aged woman at the desk. *This sweet old biddy was a madam?*

"Does it bother you, my dear?" Miss Fields asked.

"Because I can recommend another...."

June replied, "Uh, no. No, it doesn't. I've seen the other place and it's not for me." *Plus Harlin was here*, she added silently.

Miss Fields smiled prettily. "I'm so glad it doesn't, dear. You're right about the Palmer Hotel, of course. The place is a rat trap. Besides, I feel so sorry for these poor fellows, miles away from home and with no companionship. The right kind, if you know what I mean."

June smiled politely and nodded. The madam handed her a key. "Room 214, my dear. Up the stairs and to your left."

"Thank you." June started for the stairs and then remembered Harlin. "Excuse me, ma'am, but do you know what room Harlin Mason is in? I'm a friend of his and I'm supposed to meet him here."

"Of course." The older woman browsed through the hotel register. "Room 216. Just next door to you, dear. And if you want supper sent to your room, just let me know," Miss Fields added. "The food here is very good."

June smiled again. "Thank you, ma'am. I'll consider it."

After storing her gear, June stepped out into the hall and looked around. She wondered if she should look in on Harlin now or wait and ask the local marshal for help. She stopped in front of Room 216 and leaned against the door. Interesting sounds were coming from inside. The moans, a squeaking bed frame, and loud cries convinced June that Harlin was inside with someone. Probably one of Miss Fields's girls.

The sounds continued. It brought back memories of the Southern Cross. Bad memories—of Cross, Therese, Jimmy Morrow, and that bitch Ginny. And of the bastard who was responsible for that year and a half of degradation, terror, and boredom, and who was now inside the room before her, carrying on with some whore.

A hot rage engulfed June. Four years she had waited for Harlin and finally she had caught up with him. To hell with the law! She was going to bag Harlin's ass now. She knocked.

A female voice asked breathlessly, "Who is it?"

June answered, "Miss Fields told me to give a message to Mr. Mason."

The door opened slowly. "Come in."

June burst into the room, forcing a brown, shapely figure to fall to the floor with a squeal. June immediately aimed her revolver at the brown man lying in bed. *Harlin*. The anger she felt a few seconds ago subsided at the sight of the gun in his hand, aimed at her.

"Hello, Harlin," June greeted, trying to sound as calm as possible. Her heart beat rapidly.

Despite the few lines added to his face, Harlin looked as handsome as ever. Judging by the bulging muscles, he had developed his body as well. "June!" He stared at her with wide eyes. "Jesus! Never thought I'd lay eyes on you again."

"I bet you didn't." Their revolvers remained aimed at each other.

The prostitute on the floor stood up, revealing her

nakedness. Her pretty face distorted in anger, she cried, "Just who in the hell are you, busting in on my...."

"Shut up, Sue Ann!" Harlin growled. He grabbed hold of a silk robe with his free hand and threw it at the whore. "Here, put this on and go in the other room."

Sue Ann refused to move. "Why do you want to speak to her?"

Harlin's eyes became narrow as a lynx's. "Do as I say, girl, and get out!"

Her hands shaking, the prostitute put on the robe and left.

"It's been a long time, Harlin," June remarked. "Since Denver. I heard you were running from the law. What happened? That five hundred dollars ran out sooner than you thought?"

"What are you talking about?"

"Don't play with me! You sold me to Allen Cross for five hundred dollars! I was stuck in that damn whorehouse for nearly two years!"

Harlin's composure shook only slightly. "You thought I sold you to that whorehouse? Is that what this is about? Who told you? Cross? That French woman?"

June started to open her mouth to reply but kept it shut.

"Come on, Juney girl! Say something. Are you trying to tell me that you ended up working for Cross after all? Because if you are, I'll tell you right now, Cross got you for free. If they say they paid money for you, I never even seen one penny of it. I got jumped by slave catchers outside a saloon and ended on a Texas cotton plantation a couple of weeks later."

"You're lying!"

"I was stuck there till near the end of the war, when I finally managed to escape. Hell, I even went back to Denver to find you, but Cross had me thrown out. Been drifting ever since." Harlin shrugged. "Now if you want to shoot me, fine. But you'll be doing it for nothing."

A man's voice behind June added, "I doubt if she would do it for that." The cold, flat circle of a gun barrel pressed against her back.

June's heart sank.

Harlin broke into a wide smile. "Hey, Ben! It's good to see you again!"

The gun in Carlson's hand forced June farther into the room. She turned around to face the newcomer. The wanted handbills posted in the jails across the territory had not done Ben Carlson justice. He was one of the handsomest men June had ever laid eyes on, excluding Harlin. And he also possessed one of the coldest pair of gray eyes. He stood two inches shorter than Harlin and was of a slender yet wiry build.

"Who's this?" he asked Harlin. But even before Harlin mentioned June's name, she was sure there had been a flicker of recognition in Carlson's gray eyes upon sight of her. June suspected he had seen her before.

"So," Carlson continued, "your old friend tried to get the drop on you, huh?"

Harlin's eyes slowly returned to June. "Well, Juney, you gonna stand there and let Ben shoot you? Or do you wanna listen to what I have to say?"

Talking was not what June had in mind when she had arrived in Fool's Gold. But she obviously had no choice. She released a gust of breath, holstered her Colt, and sat in the nearest chair. "Okay, Harlin. Let's hear it. It's better than getting shot in the back."

Harlin then spun a tale of how he ended on a Texas cotton plantation, a month after his abduction. His second "master" had been a cruel man who made money selling his crop to the English and French through Mexico. The slaves were prevented from leaving by hired gunmen and patrollers, some who were ex-soldiers.

By the late spring of 1865, Harlin decided he had enough of his new master and Texas. One night in June, two months after Lee's surrender, Harlin managed to slip away from his cabin. He had just passed the smokehouse when he inadvertently ran into the overseer. A violent struggle occurred before Harlin stabbed the overseer to death. He then found himself wanted throughout Texas for murder and had been on the run ever since.

It was an expertly told story, incredible yet very detailed. Any person who had once been a slave would be inclined to believe it. And June almost did—until she remembered that both Harlin and Carlson had been part of Chivington's volunteer army at Sand Creek instead of in Texas. And, if his story was true, how could Harlin have known about Therese Aubry?

He had supposedly only met Cross inside the saloon.

However, the gun in Carlson's hand convinced June it was safer to believe the lie.

June feigned regret. "Harlin…, I…I didn't know. I'm sorry."

"That's OK." Harlin placed his gun in the holster hanging from the bedpost. "We've both been through a lot, so I can understand." He added with a short laugh, "Hell, I've got a mind to go after Cross myself."

"Be my guest, if you want to spend the next several years looking for him," she said. "I've had enough of hunting folks down out of vengeance."

Harlin glanced at her questioningly.

"He and Therese got kicked out of Denver a year ago," she explained.

The two former friends stared at each other for a moment, then broke into laughter. June almost forgot about Carlson. "Listen Harlin…," she began.

"I know, we need to talk. There's a restaurant across the street from the harness shop. It's called Anabelle's Kitchen. Why don't we meet there for supper? Say seven o'clock?"

"Sure. I should get back to my room." June added sardonically for Carlson's benefit, "If you don't mind."

Carlson didn't speak. He gave her a cool stare and twirled his gun expertly before slipping it into his holster.

June rolled her eyes. "Excuse me while I get ready. I'll see you and Wild Ben around seven."

158

She closed the door behind her and leaned against the wall, trembling with relief. *You stupid idiot!* she cursed herself. How could she have been so stupid as to rush in there like a hot-headed fool, thinking she could take him easily?

Levi had warned June always to confront an enemy with a cool head; it was a lesson he had drummed into her time after time. She had been careful to apply that lesson in the past year as bounty hunter. Now, when it was most important, she had allowed her anger to get the best of her, causing her to walk into a trap—a trap Harlin did not even have to set.

June admonished herself for not remembering that Barney Ward was not the only one who had been supposed to meet Harlin in Fool's Gold. Ben Carlson was a cold-blooded bastard if she had ever met one. And now she had two prairie snakes to deal with. *Jesus!*

There seemed to be only one recourse left to June: she would simply have to turn both men in to the law here in Fool's Gold. She would still have her revenge against Harlin—and her bounty.

Back outside, June led Rusty down the street in search of the marshal's office. She found that she recognized several faces in the crowds on the street. The last time she had seen them had been on wanted posters in the territory. This town was teeming with bank robbers, thieves, con-artists, murderers, and others who operated on the other side of the law! *Why wasn't the marshal doing his job and putting them behind bars? Or at least running them out of town?*

159

June came upon a large wooden building that served as a livery stable. Steaming heat blasted her face as she led Rusty inside the dimly lit structure. A burly, muscular black man with a shiny, dome-shaped head was busy shodding a horse.

"Excuse me, mister," June said. "I'd like to leave my horse here for the night."

The blacksmith glanced up and stared at June with dark eyes. "That'll be two dollars for bed and hay, miss. And an extra dollar if you want your horse shod. You'll have to wait a bit until I finish this mare."

"Fine." The man finished his job within a few minutes and took Rusty's reins. He led the horse to an empty stall. June gave him three gold coins. "By the way," she added, "you know where the marshal's office is?"

The blacksmith stared at her as if she was out of her mind. "You gotta be kidding me! What the hell you want him for? You sure ain't the law."

"Could you just tell me?"

"All right. You head west from here. It's four doors away from the Fields Hotel. Across the street from the Golden Slipper. I reckon I best warn you, if you're thinking of turning someone in, forget it."

Curious, June stared at the man. "Why?" she asked.

"Damn, girl! Don't you know where you're at? Nearly every lowlife in the territory hangs out around here without any trouble from the law! It's like a leisure spot for them. Our marshal is as crooked as the ole Mississippi. You get no trouble from him as long as you drop off a small donation on his desk. I think he's on the lam himself, if you ask me."

"Jesus Christ!"

The blacksmith peered closely at June. "You all right, girl? You look a little sick."

June sighed. Everything was going wrong. "No, it's nothing." She thanked the blacksmith for his help and left.

Now what was she going to do? Talking to the marshal was out of the question. She could contact Josh and Frank, but she did not know how long Harlin and Ben planned to stay in Fool's Gold. They might leave before the two bounty hunters could arrive. But, if she could somehow get Harlin to reveal the general location of the gold, perhaps she might be able to call on Josh and Frank for help. And Tim.

An idea began to formulate inside June's head as she returned to the hotel. On her way, she stopped at a shop and bought a dress to wear to dinner.

The noise inside Harlin's room was so loud now that she could hear it from the doorway of her room. Sue Ann must be back. June slid her key inside the lock and let herself in. Immediately, she felt a stream of warm breath upon the back of her neck.

"I thought you were going to get ready. Where have you been?" It was Ben Carlson's voice. She was so startled she nearly jumped out of her skin.

Regaining her composure, she explained that she had to put Rusty up for the night at a livery stable. "Do you always spy on people, Mr. Carlson?"

The gray eyes remained cool. "Only when that person has pulled a gun on a friend of mine. Harlin and

I always look out for each other."

"Really." Man and woman stared at each other. June had the odd feeling that Carlson's interest in her had nothing to do with suspicion. His eyes drifted toward the outline of her breasts and then returned to her eyes. June remarked, "Excuse me while I get dressed. Or do you want to watch that as well?"

Carlson smiled thinly, went out the door, and walked down the hall. June stood in her doorway and watched him enter his room. So he was attracted to her. This new twist might prove to be interesting— and very helpful.

Chapter 11

Fool's Gold, Colorado Territory, August 1868.

Two hours later, after a bath and change into the blue muslin dress she had bought on the way to her room, June met Harlin and Ben in the lobby, downstairs. The trio headed for the restaurant Harlin had mentioned earlier, Annabelle's Kitchen. The boast underneath the painted sign read: "The finest vittles served west of Denver."

Despite the crowd inside, June and Harlin were immediately led to an empty table situated near the west end of the dining room. As soon as they were seated, Harlin ordered their meal—quail, cornbread dressing and gravy, yams, and collard greens.

"You're gonna love the food here, June," Harlin said. "Miz Annabelle's one of the best cooks I've come across. She's an ex-slave from Georgia. Me and the boys ate here when she first opened. We're sor[t] of special customers."

After a brief silence, Harlin asked, "So, how long have you been looking for me?"

June told him. Although she left out Bert Todd'[s] name she recounted her departure from the Souther[n] Cross, her search for Artemus Lake, her encounter[s] with Levi Walker and Charlie Taylor, her time a[t] Lynch's station, and Levi's and Mr. Lynch's deaths. She also revealed how her bounty career had started with the search for the army deserters.

"I was the one who caught both Phil O'Keefe and Barney Ward," she said. "Not that I really wante[d] them, but I hoped they would lead me to you. It wa[s] Ward who finally told me that you and Ben would b[e] here."

"That son of a bitch!" Carlson exclaimed.

Harlin took the revelation more casually. He smile[d] wryly and said, "Barney always had a yellow streak. Always having to work up the nerve to pull a big job. Well, he's in jail now, so I reckon we don't have t[o] worry about him."

June asked, "How did you…?"

"Find myself wanted by the law?" Harlin shrugge[d] his shoulders. "When I finally escaped that Texas plantation, I stole a horse. The Texas law had a five-hundred-dollar reward on my head. I fell in with Be[n] and Phil in Fort Worth. We've been riding ever since."

Ben added, "I guess you know that we once rode with Bert Todd. Course, he's dead. Got killed i[n] Denver three years ago, the damn fool. Harlin and [I] have been running the outfit ever since."

"That explains Harlin," June said, "but not you." Her eyes examined Carlson with interest.

"Phil and I..., uh, we were serving in the army in Texas. Got fed up and deserted. We met Harlin and the three of us rode north, where we met Bert and another friend of ours, Adam Jenkins." Ben paused. "I suppose you caught him as well." His cool, gray eyes returned June's gaze with defiance.

"No. Someone beat me to him."

When the food finally arrived their conversation flagged as they concentrated on eating their meal. Harlin was right. It was the best food June had ever tasted.

Harlin asked June if she was still considering turning him and Ben over to the law in Denver. "I best warn you, this town is safe ground for outlaws. The law won't allow you to drag us out of here in chains."

"The only reason I was hunting you in the first place, Harlin, was because I thought you had sold me in Denver," June said evasively. She was finding it easier to lie. "Now that I know different, I realize I've just been wasting my time."

Harlin placed his fork on the plate. "Good, 'cause I've been thinking of something. First, how much money you got?"

"What?"

"How much money you got? I was wondering if you would like to go in business with us."

June placed her fork on her plate. "Look, I couldn't care less if you want to keep on robbing folks, but leave me...."

"No! This ain't about breaking the law. Ben and I have been thinking of starting a legitimate business. You don't mind if I talk about Bert, do you Ben?"

Harlin's friend nodded and said, "Go ahead." But he continued to eye June coolly.

June was reluctant to reveal her worth to a pair like Harlin and Carlson. She realized there was nothing they could do about it—for now. And she suspected that this was a way to get Harlin to talk about the McPherson gold.

She answered, "Twenty-eight thousand dollars. In a bank of course." Actually she had twenty thousand more, but June had decided to keep that fact to herself.

Harlin choked on the forkful of yams he had just placed in his mouth. Ben stared at her through narrowed eyes.

"Damn girl!" Harlin exclaimed after clearing his throat. "How in the hell have you managed to get so much money?"

June replied offhandedly, "I collected two thousand after working on my back for nearly two years. I got three hundred dollars for those deserters (the army's cheap), and the rest from the ten bounties I caught, including your two friends. I also invested my money in some land and a few businesses."

The two continued to stare at her with disbelief. "What are you two staring at? I figure after all the robbing you've done, you probably got twice as much."

"I only got ninety-five hundred dollars," Ben interjected.

June turned to Harlin. He replied, "About fifteen hundred."

June asked why so little.

"Oh, come on, Juney! You know me!"

"Still wasting your money, huh?" June took a bite of her dressing and quail. "You haven't changed much, Harlin."

He scowled.

"So why do you want to know how much I've got? What do you have planned?"

Harlin finished the last morsel on his plate and pushed the plate aside. "Ben and I were thinking of going straight. Start a legitimate business. Maybe a saloon or gambling hall in San Francisco. How would you like to be our partner?"

Coolly, June replied, "I'd have to be the major partner if I'd be putting up most of the cash. You two barely got half of what I'm worth."

"We'll be worth a lot more in a few days."

"What are you saying?"

June held her breath as Harlin told her about the circumstances of three years ago. It seemed, after robbing Nate McPherson of a hundred thousand in gold, Bert Todd had decided to leave no witnesses by killing him. The miner's death prompted a relentless posse to be set on the gang's trail.

"They caught up with us just a day's ride from the Wyoming border," Harlin continued. "While we were shooting it out with the posse, that double-crossing bastard Bert lit out—with our gold, we thought."

Ben picked up the tale. "When we found out that Bert got killed in Denver, we figured the law got the gold back. Turned out Bert only had a few pieces of gold on him. He had hidden the rest after walking out on us. We've kept coming back into the territory to look, but we've never found it."

After three years of going over the possibilities of the gold's location, Harlin and Ben had hit upon an idea—that Todd must have hidden the gold in the very spot where the shoot-out had occurred.

"It makes sense," Harlin insisted. "We've searched every inch of the trail between the Laramie River and Denver. It's the only place we can think of."

June looked at him. "The Laramie River? Near the fort in Wyoming?"

"No! That's the Platte. The Laramie is just below the border, at the foot of the Medicine Bow Mountains." Harlin paused for a second. He glanced at Ben and then June. "Well?"

"I don't know," June answered warily. "I mean, that money's got blood on it and I'd feel funny taking it."

Harlin squirmed in his seat impatiently. "Look, I admit that the fellow we stole it from was killed. But it was that crazy fool Bert who did it."

June remained silent.

"Jesus, girl! It's been three years! I bet hardly no one remember that damn gold anymore!"

Except Tim, June responded silently. "But what do you need me for? You'll have enough once you find it."

"I don't know. I guess seeing you again. After all, we're old friends."

"And just in case you don't find it, you'll have my money to back you up—and me not to tell anyone where you are."

Harlin laughed. Ben just looked at her with a faint smile on his lips.

"That's what I've always liked about you, June. You're the sharpest little thing on two legs." His brown eyes glittered with excitement as he leaned forward. "Now, how about it?"

"Well...."

"Not many people think of bounty hunting as a respectable profession, do they? And you only did it to find me. Well, now that you have, what are you going to do next?"

June finished the last of her quail and dressing. "I see your point," she finally conceded, thinking she had strung Harlin along far enough. "I might as well go with you. Hell, I've got nothing better to do."

Slapping the table in good humor, Harlin called for the waiter. While his face was averted, June's eyes met Ben's across the table.

Harlin told her they would be leaving for their trip north the next day. He and Ben deposited her at the hotel so that she could go to her room and go to bed. When she spotted them entering a saloon, she made her way to the telegraph office. One telegram was wired to Joshua Walker and Frank Spencer, now living at a newly built town in Wyoming Territory called

169

Cheyenne. She left them instructions to meet her near the location Harlin had mentioned. Realizing that the two might be after another bounty, she sent a second telegram to Tim McPherson in Denver.

June sighed and hoped that somebody would reach her in time. She did not want them to find her body somewhere on the road to California.

June had just returned to the hotel when she spotted a familiar figure heading toward her. She rushed inside so that Ben Carlson would not see her and ask why she had gone back outside. Unfortunately, as she was heading up the staircase, he entered the lobby.

"June!" he cried out. The outlaw hurried to June's side. "What are you doing up? I thought you went to bed."

"I wasn't sleepy, so I decided to take a walk," June replied shortly, annoyed that she had been seen on the street. "Where's Harlin, by the way? Wasn't he with you?"

Ben grimaced. "He got into a card game, as usual. I didn't feel like watching him lose the last of his money."

June smiled. "And I thought Harlin had gotten over that bad habit by now. I see you know how to hold on to your money."

"Yeah, well I've always been careful. Something none of the others were capable of. At least Harlin knew how to plan a robbery. Bert was more reckless. He'd get this crazy notion in his head and wouldn't let go. I guess robbing came a lot easier to us."

"I wouldn't say that, considering your unfortunate choice of partners."

The pair stopped in front of June's hotel room and faced each other. "Maybe it's time I get myself a new one. A person who can hold onto her money, who has a good head on her shoulders." His eyes pierced June's like a sharp knife.

June stared back. Here comes the proposition. "What are you trying to say?"

"I'm trying to say," Carlson's hand lightly caressed June's shoulder, "why don't we take that gold for ourselves? Start a business in Frisco together."

June slowly removed his hand from her shoulder. She turned around and unlocked her door. "You'd cheat your best friend?"

"He was your best friend, too, but that didn't stop him from selling you to that whorehouse in Denver. I should know; I helped him."

June's eyes narrowed dangerously.

"Oh, come on! You really didn't believe that tale of his? Hell, he just borrowed the story of what happened to Adam Jenkins, one of our partners. Back in '64, Harlin and I had joined...."

"Chivington's bunch," June finished for him. Ben stared at her. "I heard you two were selling scalps on the streets after Sand Creek."

Ben broke into laughter. "Well, I'll be damned! You've known all along!" Then his laughter subsided. "That means you're still after Harlin!"

"That's right."

"You plan to take me in as well?"

June's eyes flickered as she gave him a cryptic smile. "I was thinking of it. Of course, I now realize it would be in the best interest of my health to concern myself only with Harlin."

"He ain't never gonna let you take him in alive. You'll have to kill him."

"I reckon." June remained cool.

"So why not join up with me? With our money combined, we'll make a damn good team. Like that Cross fellow and his French woman." Ben managed to ease himself into her room.

His hand returned to June's shoulder. Slowly it traveled up toward her neckline, then downward again and cupped her left breast. June realized that Carlson was a dangerous man, but she found his touch physically tantalizing. She stepped closer, breathing hard.

"Mix a little business with pleasure, while we're at it," he added.

"Maybe." His thumb began to circle the tip of her nipple. "Let me think on it first. After all, I hardly know you. And since I don't," June removed his hand from her breast, reluctantly, "I suggest you ask that nice Miz Fields for a night companion."

Before June could protest further, Ben crushed her mouth with his and kissed her hard and long. Between ragged breaths, he said, "That was just to let you know what you can look forward to if you take up my offer." He smiled briefly and opened the door. "Good night," he said and left.

June encountered her two new companions at

breakfast the next morning at Annabelle's Kitchen. Harlin was busy wolfing down a plate of eggs, potatoes, sausage, and biscuits. Ben, she saw, only allowed himself a cup of coffee. He was trying his best to stifle a yawn.

"Good morning, you two." June sat down in the empty chair at the table. A waiter immediately appeared at her side. She ordered fried potatoes, toast, and coffee. Ben yawned again. "Didn't get enough sleep?" she asked with a sly smile. It appeared that Ben had taken her suggestion last night.

Ben peered at her through heavy-lidded eyes. "Just barely."

"You should have stayed at the saloon with me, Ben," Harlin remarked. "I won fifteen hundred dollars last night at poker."

June smiled at her old friend. "Congratulations, Harlin. I bet this must be a first for you."

"Not really. Sometimes I win, but rarely."

Ben yawned again. Harlin looked at him. "Damn, boy! You're hardly awake! Why don't you go back to the hotel and get some shut-eye. We won't be leaving until noon anyway."

Ben drained the last of his coffee. "Sounds like a good idea. At least I'll have another three hours of sleep." He got up from his chair and left.

Harlin and June watched him leave before Harlin said to her, "You two must have had a good time last night." Harlin's comment took June by surprise. "Course, he doesn't exactly strike me as your type."

"I didn't sleep with him. I suggested he find someone else for the night. How did you know he was in my room?"

"One of Miz Fields's girls told me." Harlin suddenly leaned forward. "Don't get too close with him, Juney; that boy's a cold fish."

"I thought he was your friend."

"Sure he is. Sort of. That don't mean I trust him completely. A man or a woman has to be careful around the likes of Ben. He'll stick around only as long as he thinks it'll do him any good."

For a moment, June wondered if Harlin would believe her if she revealed how his friend was prepared to betray him. It gave her an idea.

"If you don't trust him that much, why stay with him?" June asked. "Why don't you two just split up after you find the gold? Or better yet, keep the gold for yourself?"

June held her breath as Harlin contemplated what she had said. Slowly, his dark eyes met hers. "Ben has been my riding partner for a long time. I couldn't cheat him out of his share of the gold."

"Why not? He's planning to do that to you."

Harlin stiffened. "What are you talking about?"

With great relish, June told him of the discussion between her and Carlson—with a few alterations. Instead of revealing her intentions to turn Harlin in, she credited Ben with the idea.

Harlin stared at her with disbelief. "I can't see Ben double-crossing me, especially when he hardly knows you. Even if you are a female."

"What about my twenty-eight thousand dollars?

It'll come in handy, especially if you don't find this gold. And I don't intend to touch it until after I reach Frisco and have it wired to me."

"That'd do it all right. The son of a bitch!"

"So? What are going to do about him?" June looked at Harlin intently.

A slow smile stretched across Harlin's face. "Let him keep thinking he's going to get the drop on me. And when he makes his move," he turned to face June, "we'll make ours."

The tension inside June slowly dissipated as she observed Harlin's grim smile. Everything was going just as she had hoped. Somewhere along the banks of the Laramie River, one man would betray a four-year friendship and help June collect a ten-thousand-dollar bounty and revenge.

While Harlin stopped at a dry goods store on the way back to the hotel, June went to Ben's room to wake him up. She found the outlaw wide awake.

"We're getting ready to leave soon," June said after he opened the door. Ben was fully dressed except for a shirt. "I just came to see if you were awake."

June turned to leave, but suddenly Ben gripped her arm and dragged her inside the room. He closed the door behind her and pressed her against the wall. "Well, have you made a decision?" His two wiry arms straddled the sides of her shoulders.

"I only have one question," June answered. "How do I know you won't double-cross me like you're about to do with Harlin?"

175

Ben smiled. "You don't. Sorry, honey, but that's the best answer I can give you. You don't know, and I don't know if you'll do the same to me. But that's what's going to make our partnership interesting, don't you think?"

"Rather dangerous if you ask me."

"So what? I reckon you wouldn't mind the danger. If you didn't, you wouldn't have become a bounty hunter in the first place."

June laughed softly. "You know me that well, do you?"

"No, but I've got a good idea of what you're like." Ben leaned forward and brushed the side of her neck with his lips. "Now, what's your answer going to be?" His lips slowly traveled toward her mouth and began to nibble her lower lip.

June's breathing became ragged. Why did this man have to be so damned attractive? She was almost tempted to give in to his suggestion. *Almost.* "Uh...."

Ben finally kissed her fully on the mouth, driving all thoughts from her mind except for the hard, masculine body that pressed her against the wall.

Ben lifted his head. "Well?"

"All right, I'm in. But we find the gold before we get rid of him."

"Whatever you say, sweetheart." They threw themselves into each other's arms and continued their passionate embrace.

The trio said their good-byes to the diminutive Miss Fields and set out for the trail around one in the afternoon. As their horses trudged through the muddy streets, June asked Harlin if he was sure he knew where the gold was.

"Don't worry. I have a pretty good idea where it is," Harlin answered in typically enigmatic fashion. "As soon as we dig it up, we'll be on our way to California and have ourselves a fine saloon or gambling hall. How do you like that?"

"As long as we don't run a whorehouse," June answered. "I had enough of that back in Denver. If you want, you can get someone else to run one for you."

Harlin laughed and Ben smiled. "You don't have to worry about that, Juney. I doubt if we'll even open one. I don't know about Ben, but I'm tired of having the law breathing down my back. We can make a fortune with just a gambling house."

"And maybe a restaurant," Ben added. "June can run that while we run the tables."

Harlin and Ben went on about the opportunities available in California. The way the two were talking, June considered, they thought they were on the way to a second gold rush.

Other thoughts nagged June as they rode north along the foothills. Like where was this gold? Although they had only been in the saddle for less than a day, June hoped the journey would not take too long. For the first time in over a year, the patience she had acquired was receding.

She was also leery of being in Harlin's and Ben's company. As she had done back in Fool's Gold, June

177

regretted her hasty actions that first day at the Fields Hotel. She should have kept her distance and trailed the pair. Instead, she was riding with them. And something always went wrong whenever she traveled with a companion. There had been problems when she was first with Harlin, then with Levi and the Lynches, and finally with Charlie. June feared disaster awaited her on this trip.

Carlson presented another problem. Judging by the way he glanced at her, June guessed he could not wait to get under her pants. And she feared that she would not resist much when he tried. How was it that a cool customer like Ben Carlson could be so randy?

After the trio had set camp after the second day on the trail, Harlin went off to hunt game for supper. Finding a secluded spot in a stream between several boulders, June started to undress for a quick bath. She got as far as removing her blouse when a pair of steel arms caught her by surprise.

"Jesus, man!" she exclaimed as Ben planted kisses along the back of her neck. "You're just about the randiest tomcat I've ever met!"

Slowly, Ben's fingers began to unfasten the buttons to her chemise. "Oh c'mon, June. Harlin's going to be away for a while. What's wrong with a little fun?" He spun her around and started nibbling her exposed cleavage. As before, June found him hard to resist.

"Lord help me when you finally get tired of me."

Ben lifted his head. "Ah, hell! That won't make me give up a profitable partnership. My uncle once told me never to mix business with pleasure. He should know; he owned a whorehouse and tavern in Evansville for years. He raised me."

That explained his technique with women, June thought. Young Ben must have learned a few other lessons while living in that place.

"And what are you doing now?" she asked in ragged breath.

"Pleasure." His mouth continued to caress June's upper chest.

To June's relief, she heard hoofbeats in the distance. She started to push the outlaw away. "Ben, we have to stop."

"Why?"

The two heard a loud greeting. Harlin had returned to camp.

Ben muttered, "Shit," and released June.

After that incident, June made sure she was never alone with Ben again.

One other worry plagued her. Had Josh, Frank, and Tim receive their telegrams in time? June hoped so. The possibility that the friends might be faking their betrayal nagged at the back of June's mind. If that were the case, she would eventually have hell to pay with the two outlaws.

On the third day, June, Harlin, and Ben reached the foothills of the Medicine Bow Mountains. Below them, the Laramie River shimmered like a silvery ribbon across the terrain. Harlin spread his arms out. "Well, we're here."

They were there all right, June thought—*with no*

sign of Josh, Frank, or Tim. Dammit! She remained calm and asked, "So, where's the gold?"

Harlin and Ben glanced about. Harlin strode toward a hollow in the ground, surrounded by large rocks. He stood next to a small boulder. "I think this is where Bert was during that shoot-out. Right, Ben?"

Ben shrugged his shoulders. "Don't ask me. I was too busy trying to keep that posse away from us. All I know is that I was over here." He stood a few feet away from Harlin, next to a larger rock.

June glanced up. Dark, threatening rain clouds formed above. *Oh, wonderful!* she thought moodily. *That's all I need right now. Rain!*

Harlin knelt down and examined the ground. "Hey! I was right! Look!" He held up a bent silver locket. "A girl back in Julesburg gave it to Bert, remember? It was his lucky piece."

"It must have been," Ben replied. "He sure didn't have much luck after he lost it." The loud rumble of thunder punctuated his comment.

Harlin pushed aside the small boulder next to him. He thrust an arm into the ground and pulled something out. "Look at what we got here!" Clutched in Harlin's fist was a bulging, thick burlap sack. He broke into a triumphant grin.

June stared at the sack with wide eyes. "How much is there, you reckon?"

"Forty thousand dollars, and it's all ours."

"You mean mine and June's," Ben remarked. "And now," he uncocked the Colt revolver in his right hand and aimed it at Harlin, "I think we'll be taking it."

Chapter 12

Medicine Bow Mountains, Colorado Territory, September 1868.

June followed Ben's example and drew her gun. Harlin stared at his partners as if unsure whether this was a joke or real. "What the hell is this?"

"What does it look like? We're double-crossing you. By the way, you mind doing me a favor by dropping your gun belt."

Harlin slowly unbuckled his gun belt and let it slide to the ground.

"Why did you...?" Harlin began.

"Decide to take the money for ourselves? When June here remarked about the money she had back in Denver, I came to realize that she would make a better partner. She doesn't piss her money away on cards and such like you do. You were a good partner in crime, Harlin. But as for one in business...." Ben shook his head.

He continued, "By the way, did you know that she never believed that cock-and-bull story of yours about Texas? She knows what we did to her back in Denver."

Harlin stared at June, a look of horror in his eyes. She remained calm, her revolver still aimed at him.

Harlin's face twisted in rage. "You stupid bitch!" he bellowed. "You can't possibly still believe that! I tried to explain!"

Carlson continued, amused by his ex-partner's outburst. "Course, it was your idea. Personally, I can't understand why you didn't stick with her. She's a hell of a lot more interesting than that cheap whore, Sue Ann. And smarter. Unfortunate for you," he extended his gun arm at Harlin, "you discovered too late."

Taking the outlaw by surprise, June aimed her gun and shot Ben's revolver out of his hand. Stunned, he looked at June. His former partner quickly drew a deadly-looking bowie knife. Ben stumbled backward, afraid.

Harlin grinned wickedly. "You know, for a smart man, Ben, you're really stupid. Did you really think she would believe your lies? It was nice knowing you." He suddenly threw himself against Ben and, with a grunt, shoved the knife into his partner's stomach. Eyes bugged out, Ben stumbled a few steps forward and sank to the ground.

Harlin spit on the corpse and picked up his gun. "Now that the son of a bitch is dead, we can...." He stopped in mid-sentence. June's Colt revolver remained in her hand and was now aimed at Harlin's chest.

Harlin's face became rigid as she faced him coldly. "Damn, Juney, don't tell me you believe what...."

"Don't say another word," June interrupted. "I don't want to hear it."

Harlin began to plead. "Come on, gal. Ben was lying! Like I told you, I got sent to Texas!"

"Shut up! You weren't in Texas during the last year of the war. A customer at the Southern Cross described you and Ben as two of Chivington's volunteers. And both of you seemed to know about Therese. I didn't meet her until after I was kidnapped."

June uncocked her gun. "You know, it's a good thing you're wanted dead or alive. I reckon I'd have a hard time taking you in breathing. Bye, Harlin."

"All right! I admit it! I was desperate for money and you weren't willing to work for Cross!" Harlin cried desperately. "Hell, you shouldn't be upset! You earned a lot of money, didn't you?"

June's eyes narrowed as she extended her gun arm. "You son of a bitch! Who do you think I am? Your mother?"

For a brief second, a glint of hatred shone in Harlin's eyes. Then he resumed his pleading. "Jesus, please! No! Look, I'll make it up to you! You can have the gold, just let me go!"

Tears began to form in Harlin's eyes. June couldn't believe it. It was disgusting! Didn't the man have any pride? She sighed, suddenly feeling a wash of sympathy for her old friend. Watching Harlin beg for his life reminded her of when she had begged Cross and Therese for hers. "All right." She lowered her gun. "Jesus Christ! Stop begging, Harlin!"

Harlin wiped his tears away.

"Just get out of here! I don't want to see you again!"

He continued to stand there, looking like a sad-eyed idiot. Disgusted, June turned around and started toward Rusty. *Oh God*, she suddenly thought, *his gun. She forgot to take his gun.*

First there was a click, followed by a gunshot. June grunted as a fiery pain pierced her left shoulder. She fell backward, slamming against Rusty. Her Colt remained in her right hand. "Sorry, June honey," a cooler Harlin said, "but you shouldn't have made that remark about my mother. And you should have put Denver behind…."

June swiveled around like a whip and shot Harlin in the chest. His eyes widened in disbelief. "Jesus," he muttered.

"Good-bye, Harlin." She fired a second shot, this one in the head, killing Harlin instantly. Another rumble of thunder announced a heavy downpour of rain.

June stared at Harlin's corpse, her own body rapidly becoming soaked from the rain. But she did not cry. She felt nothing. Instead, she shivered from the wet rain. How long had they known each other? Seventeen years. She had been five and he eight. To her, the Harlin she had known had died in Denver four years ago. She remembered how she had wept upon discovering what he had done. But she did not weep now.

The gold. She had to get the…. Everything started to spin in circles. God, she was getting dizzy. June started for the sacks of gold near the hollow. The pain in her shoulder intensified and her vision became blurred. She bent over to pick up the sack and blacked out.

June slowly opened her eyes. Two, no, three faces focused into view—two brown and one white.

"She's finally awake," a familiar voice said.

"Charlie?" June asked. *What was Charlie doing in Colorado?*

She finally saw his face in a clear, sharp image. And standing right behind him were Josh Walker and Frank Spencer. "Charlie, what the hell are you doing here? What happened to me?"

Charlie leaned forward and kissed her forehead. "Don't try to move, June. You've lost a lot of blood. The doc said you should be OK in a few days."

Still, June tried to sit up. She felt a sharp pain in her shoulder. Defeated, she slumped back onto the bed. "You still haven't explained what you're doing here. Where am I?"

Josh leaned forward. "Fort Collins. We found you near the Laramie River, west of here."

"There were two other bodies there," she began to explain. "Harlin and…."

"We found Mason and Carlson. And the gold too." Josh smiled. "I see you didn't need our help after all."

June muttered, "I don't know about that. If you had been around, I probably wouldn't have been shot."

Frank Spencer added, "Well, no matter now. Those two boys are worth five thousand dollars apiece. That's ten thousand for you. The folks here have them stored in the old guard house until you can take them back to Denver."

June remained silent.

"June?" Joe added. "What's wrong? You upset about Harlin? I know he was your friend and all...."

"It's not just that," June interrupted. "I was wondering. All those years I thought about getting revenge. Four long years. And now that he's dead, I don't know what to do next. The fever's gone."

The three men in the room did not speak. They stood above the bed, staring at the empty expression in her eyes.

Within four days, June recovered from her wounds and was ready to leave for Denver. It was time Tim McPherson got his gold back.

She announced her intentions to Charlie one evening as they walked down the main street of Fort Collins. Until a year ago, the town had been an army post guarding the Overland Trail until the military had decided to abandon it.

Joe remained silent. "You never did tell me how you got here," June said in an attempt to break his silence.

Charlie explained that he had gone to Denver on a furlough to see June. "I was at your boardinghouse when your telegram for that McPherson fellow arrived."

"But I sent it to Tim's house."

"He was out of town, so his housekeeper gave it to Miss Jackson. I ran into Josh and that friend of his in town."

"Oh."

The uncomfortable silence returned. The two stared at the mountains beyond the horizon.

June then asked, "Why did you come to Denver?"

"To ask you to marry me," Charlie replied quietly. Stunned, June faced him and stared. "Yeah, I still want you for my wife, despite what you told me last year."

"Charlie...."

"After Ellsworth, I couldn't stop thinking about you. And like you said, now that Harlin's dead, you have nothing else to do. You can now be my wife."

June looked deeply into those hazel brown eyes. She had to admit that she did love Charlie. In a certain way. He would make a fine husband and maybe they could create a marriage together, despite what Levi Walker had once said.

"All right, Charlie, I'll marry you. But...." Charlie smiled with relief and hugged June. "But I won't be an army wife. I meant what I said last year." The smile disappeared. The howl of a coyote pierced the still air.

"You mean you want me to leave the army?"

"Yes."

"It's my life, June. It's where I belong."

"I don't feel as you do, Charlie. I've never liked the army. Not during the war and certainly not now."

Charlie's face deepened into a scowl. "What the hell's wrong with it? I know it ain't perfect, but what you do ain't either."

A slow anger surged inside June. Was he referring to the Southern Cross? "What's that supposed to mean?" she snapped.

"Bounty hunting! Chasing down men and turning them in for money. You might as well be some damn vulture!"

"At least I've been earning money for myself. Using my wits! Not taking orders from some idiots and killing Indians!"

"June!"

"Is that what you want to do, Charlie? Spend the rest of your life getting paid thirteen dollars a month to help the government steal land from others?"

"It's the same government that freed our people!"

"So what am I supposed to do? Be grateful for the rest of my life? Hell, back in Tennessee, they wanted us to stay on that damn plantation so we could grow cotton for them! Wards of the government! I might as well have remained as George Devon's slave!"

"June," Charlie said hoarsely.

It was no use, June thought. *Charlie would be unhappy if he left the army. He loved it too much. And if she married him, it would be a war between her and the army for the rest of his life. And she would lose.*

June sighed. "Charlie, we best forget marriage. I don't think it would work. We both want different things."

Accusing eyes bored into hers. "So what are you going to do, continue being a bounty hunter?" Charlie stood defiantly before her.

"Might as well," June replied mournfully. "It's what I do best. Bye, Charlie." She turned around and walked back toward the doctor's office.

The next morning, June discovered that Josh and Frank had decided to accompany her to Denver. "What for?" she protested at the breakfast table. "I won't be in any danger."

Josh patiently explained that she was carrying forty thousand dollars in gold stolen from Tim's brother. It was enough money to attract any road agent on the trail.

"I don't need your protection!"

"I swear to God, you are the most pig-headed woman I have ever met! June, we're going with you, whether you like it or not. Even if it means following you without you knowing it. Right, Frank?"

The Georgian smiled, seemingly amused by the couple's dispute. "He's right. You won't be safe carrying that gold by yourself."

"Pig-headed, am I?" June glared at Josh. "All right! Meet me inside the livery stable after dinner. Jesus!" Then she stalked out of the room.

At the appointed hour, the three bounty hunters stood inside the livery stable, preparing for the trip south. The bodies of Harlin and Ben had been placed in a wagon June had bought from the stable's owner.

She had just finished tying Rusty to the back when she looked up and saw Charlie standing in the doorway. He had not appeared at breakfast.

"Charlie?"

The trooper stood awkwardly, dressed in civilian clothes. "I won't be heading back for Kansas until tomorrow and I wanted to say good-bye. And apologize for yesterday."

"You have nothing to apologize for," June said softly. A lump formed in her throat.

He held out his right hand. "We're still friends, aren't we?"

An enigmatic smile appeared on June's lips as she walked toward him. "You know that, Charlie Taylor! We're more than just friends." She leaned forward and kissed him fully on the lips. They finally parted after a few minutes.

"I guess you're right," he muttered. Charlie kissed June again. Longer. "Bye, June."

"Bye, Charlie. You take care of yourself."

June watched as his figured merged into the sunlight outside and disappeared.

Someone's throat cleared. June had forgotten the two bounty hunters behind her. Josh was busy focusing his attention on the opposite wall. Frank seemed more interested in the scene that had just occurred.

"Ready to ride?" The Georgian asked her.

June nodded. She climbed aboard the wagon. The two men mounted their horses. The trio rode out of the stable.

"Say, June, Josh and I wondered if you would still

consider becoming our partner?" Frank asked as they rode away from town.

"Don't be insulted, but the answer's no."

"Why not? What's wrong with us?"

"Nothing. It's just that I'm too used to riding alone. And I don't like splitting the reward money."

"Well, that's pretty damn selfish!"

"But," June continued in an attempt to be conciliatory, "maybe I'll take up your offer one of these days."

Josh snorted and muttered, "Horse shit!"

June glanced at him sharply. "I beg your pardon?"

"I said 'horse shit.' I bet you're not that used to riding alone. You're just uncomfortable with the thought of working with another person again."

June opened her mouth.

"But that's okay. Frank and I can wait." Josh smiled pleasantly.

Smart ass! she thought angrily, upset that he had accurately guessed the reason behind her decision. And Levi once thought she and this man would make a great couple! Hah! She threw Josh a fierce glare as she urged the team of horses to turn south. The two men followed and they all set off on their journey to Denver.

191

FREEDOM RUN

By Rina Keaton

When Armand Vernier dies in 1845, his sons betray his will and sell their mulatto half sister, Janine, into slavery. Her brother and mother escape to Canada. Eventually they persuade an Englishman, Steven Williams, and his friend,

Jerome Trent, posing as Steven's slave, to undertake a daring rescue of Janine and her friend Claudia. As they make their way north by steamboat, Janine poses as Steven's wife, and Claudia as her maid. Still, time after time, they have to use their wits and cunning to elude the slave catchers sent to recapture them. Author Rina Keaton paints a vivid picture of both the charm and the horror of the Old South.

"*Freedom Run* is a page turner! The ending will leave you smiling with delight!"

HOLLOWAY HOUSE PUBLISHING COMPANY
8060 Melrose Avenue, Los Angeles, CA 90046